Pale With Color

by

Susan JP Owens

I hope you enjoy reading my story as much as I loved writing it!

All the Best,

Susan JP Owens

This is a work of fiction. Names, characters, places, and incidents are either the product of the author's imagination or are used fictitiously, and any resemblance to actual persons living or dead, business establishments, events, or locales, is entirely coincidental.

Pale With Color

Copyright 2015 by Susan JP Owens

All rights reserved. No part of this book may be used or reproduced in any manner whatsoever without written permission of the authors except in the case of brief quotations embodied in critical articles or reviews.

Cover Art by Diana Carlile
http://www.designingdiana.blogspot.com

Published in the United States of America

Dedication

Jimmy, thank you for your unwavering support.

Chapter One

Cheyenne Clark stood on her tiptoes and peeked over one spectator's shoulder, then another. If she wanted to see the Civil War reenactment, she'd have to find a different spot. Off to the left side of the field, woods delineated a well-defined edge and nestled beside it was an outcropping of rocks with a lone tree several feet forward from the border. She headed toward the shade.

The clouds had covered the sky earlier, but now the sun shined. Odd no one else had claimed a place under the lush canopy because the oppressive heat rose in constant waves. People from across the country and around the world entered the National Military Park to watch the annual Battle of Gettysburg recreated. She scanned the horizon; she'd be in an excellent position to see the fight for Wheatfield unfold.

She withdrew a quilt from her backpack and placed the cover on the grass. Settled on the blanket, she opened a bottle of water and guzzled. Somehow she and her best friend had crossed wires, and Bethany ended up at Culp's Hill. They had each chosen to stay where they were so she had plenty of munchies and drinks until the end of the day.

Her cell phone chimed the distinctive tone for a message. She grabbed her mobile, swiped the screen, tapped the password and then waited. "My Indian Princess." *What the...?* The words were backward, and obviously someone had the wrong number or instead of the infamous butt call, maybe it was a butt text. She pressed the home button and stuffed the phone into her back pocket.

A white arc flickered across her face. She ducked from the unpleasant glare. Inching her gaze toward the cause, she searched for the offending reason. A man stood on the outskirts of the crowd observing her, and the pendent on his necklace reflected the sun's rays. His eyes locked with hers. Goose bumps rose over her skin and chills scurried down her spine because there was a recognition of some kind. Odd, she couldn't put her finger on why, but his gaze was enough to rattle her. She broke eye contact, then glanced back, and he was gone. How bizarre. She shrugged and dismissed the peculiar feelings.

A bugle sounded and the charge commenced with the well-known Rebel yells, she shuddered from the loud screams. The thick smoke rose as each weapon fired, and the artillery expelled the black powder with each horrendous boom. Within minutes, the stench of gunpowder engulfed her surroundings. Her eyes and nose burned. She wrapped a scarf around her face and slid on her sunglasses.

Earlier in the morning, the re-enactors portrayed the renewed attack at Culp's and Cemetery Hill. Also, they had played out the scene where Mary Virginia "Jenny" Wade was shot in town by a stray bullet. The actors used stage blood for a realistic visual. She could've done without the added graphics, but the pictorial did the job on her stomach. After popping several antacids, her tummy had calmed.

Her arm jostled. "Yes?" She twisted to her right. Bethany must have come back to join her.

"What in God's name are you doing here? You have a death wish?" The irritated bass voice demanded an answer.

"This was the coolest area to watch...as in more comfortable." She notched her chin several inches higher and defended the position because she was within the boundary markers.

"If you like to observe men die, I can give you an eye full. Come to think of it, you may be the type of person I need. My men are stretched thin and I don't have any extra help. I've been told the townspeople have their hands full." His tall frame folded lower into a squat.

Type? "I'm not dressed for the reenactment." She whipped off her glasses and slid the makeshift mask to her neck.

"I don't care how you're dressed. Some of these soldiers will have half a chance of surviving, if you can assist me." His apron outlined an expansive chest and dripped with fake blood.

Surviving? A tiny bit melodramatic? "I've acted before at community theatres so I shouldn't embarrass you too bad. I can cover for a little bit. At least until the person I'm filling in for gets here." She stood and he yanked her to her knees. "What the—"

"When you rise, stay hunkered down. By the

way, I could use your blanket." He rose and bent at his waist, pivoted toward the woods, then turned back. "Bring your things. We'll be a while." He paused for a brief second. When he exhaled, his emerald eyes seemed sad and exhausted. "Forgive my manners. My name is Captain Joseph Westerly. We're informal with civilians during these times. Call me Joseph."

"Cheyenne Clark." She offered her hand for a polite shake.

His brows furrowed, and he spread his arms wide to display the blood on his frame. "As you can see for yourself, you shouldn't touch me. Follow me." His finger pointed to a path beyond the boulders.

"Nice to meet you, too." She jammed her water bottle into the nylon backpack and slung one strap over her shoulder. In one deft motion, she gathered the quilt and trailed behind one super good looking Captain Westerly, who carried out his job way too passionately. Although he still had another day of acting, he appeared too fatigued to continue.

Most men had grown long and unkempt beards and mustaches, but Joseph's shadow of blond facial hair stirred heat between her legs. Yummy, she liked guys with barely there scruffy beards like they had just awakened. Joseph's fingernails were well-groomed and clean. His pruned skin looked as though he'd been washing dishes for the last twenty-four hours, and he had a jagged scar on his left ring finger.

The reenactments were taken in earnest; everything was to the time period specs, clothes, weapons, artillery, right down to the shelter halves, tents for the officers, and utensils.

She especially liked the evening, when they allowed the spectators to mingle with the soldiers at their respective camps to get a firsthand view of how the men lived during war time. Most of the participants enjoyed sharing the way of life with the audiences and had fun. However, Joseph took his acting stint a bit too seriously.

As she entered the woods, Union men rushed past her with the wounded, some of the injured hung over their shoulders while others were on improvised stretchers. Loud groans added to the din of the battle. The odor of blood, sweat and gunpowder residue overwhelmed her. Her eyes watered, and her stomach lurched. The pungent aromas that assailed her nostrils were too realistic. Whoever the organizers were for the field hospital certainly did a good job in the olfactory department.

"Miss Clark, put your knapsack there." The captain hunched over a soldier on a makeshift table bobbed his head in the general direction of a canvas tent. Westerly must be portraying a doctor.

"Call me Cheyenne." She dropped her things and looked past the singular tree where she agreed to playact. The authentic recreation continued while mesmerized onlookers stood on the sidelines. In the distance, RVs, cars, and motorcycles packed the parking lots. Why was everything opposite of where she remembered? Oh well, the people might have relocated as the fight for control shifted, and as for the parking lots, obviously she hadn't paid attention.

Cognizant of her straying thoughts, she turned back to the stage area of the field hospital. Caretakers scurried from one patient to the next as the wounded begged for help, water or both. Of course, she could pretend to aid the actors. She'd bet her last dollar they'd appreciate a drink in this stifling heat and humidity.

She spied the bucket with the ladle and scooped the container in her hand. The injured laid wherever there was a vacant spot, and as far as she could see, there wasn't an unoccupied piece of ground available. She knelt, cupped the first one's head, and trickled the clear liquid into his mouth. He looked far too young to be portraying a soldier. If this boy was a day over thirteen, she'd eat her scarf.

A man's scream riveted her attention to Joseph's table. She didn't have any medical training, but without a doubt, he represented a surgeon finished with an amputation. Her insides somersaulted. She gaped, repulsed by how accurate the setting revealed all of the trauma each man endured.

"Don't stand there with your mouth open. Clean this man while I stitch." He washed his hands with lye soap and a brush, then dried them on a torn piece of material which looked like an old petticoat. According to what she had learned, during this era, most doctors were unaware of the correlation between sanitation and germs. Ha, good old Joseph wasn't keeping to era specifications.

"I get sick putting a Band-Aid on my finger." Where was Bethany when she needed her? Bethany was the physician's assistant. Cheyenne traipsed to the table, snatched several long pieces of an underskirt and studied the soldier. Sweat, dirt and blood dribbled down his face and, his clothes were a mess. She wiped the grit, and then cradled his head and gave him water.

"Thank you ma'am." The man's eyes appeared appreciative before they glazed over and he passed out.

Wow, these actors were good. Time to perform and not disappoint ol' Joseph and the rest of the players. She examined the wound, exposed bone and torn tissue from the saw hung from the stump.

"My God, this is real." Dread filled her stomach like she swallowed ten pounds of lead. She dashed over to the men lying on the ground and checked one, then another. Fear escalated to terror. She assessed one more and spun to Joseph. "These are actual wounds. We've got to stop them. Someone is using real ammo."

Her vision blurred as her legs gave out. Collapsing onto the ground, she gasped for air. She inhaled several times. When her ability to see returned, she snatched her cell and dialed 9-1-1. Nothing. She checked the strength of the signal. Zilch. Cheyenne fought to rise. Joseph lightly grasped her arm. With his support, she stood, and her dizziness disappeared.

"We've got to stop them." She yanked free from his clasp and ran toward the open field. Her adrenaline pumped and her heart pounded, but her feet were heavy and out of sync with her brain. Finally, clearing the tree line, she passed the mighty oak that had once given her shade before this horrible disaster occurred.

"We need doctors. Nurses. EMTs. Anyone." She stumbled and regained her balance.

"Get down." Joseph tackled her to the ground. His entire frame covered hers. She grunted under his weight and lifted her gaze to the hazy smoke swirling around the battlefield. Union and Confederates soldiers fell like rag dolls.

Her mobile lay lopsided beside her head in the tall grass. She checked the face. Black. "What in the world is going on?" Did her phone break from hitting the ground? She confronted Joseph's scowl. "Would you get off me? I need to find the organizers and tell them someone added real ammo."

"You're psychotic. If I can't get you behind those boulders, you're going to get us killed." He growled between taking a mouthful of air and a snarl punctuated the end.

"I'm not hallucinating. The actors can't hear us over the barrage of explosions so we need to get to the spectators." She pointed. "Maybe their cell phones are working."

His line of sight followed the path of her finger, then she readjusted because they should've been standing to her right, and they were on her left. Joseph's head shook slowly, his pitying gaze returned.

"All I see are opposing regiments fighting. Each man killing each other for their own reasons." His final words lowered to a mere whisper.

"Gettysburg had the most casualties of the Civil War, but that doesn't mean the actors should actually die. We've got to help."

She clutched his chin and thrust his face in the direction of the parking lots. "Can you see the RV's and the cars?"

When he cleared his throat, she released her hold. His gaze reconnected. "I don't know what those are." As he exhaled a lengthy breath, compassion mixed with concern emanated from his eyes.

"You don't know what they…" Her mind struggled to comprehend the anomaly. This was like an episode from a sci-fi movie. Could she have entered a time warp, and she was the only witness? The era would explain the cause of her phone not working, possibly why everything was backward and the ghastly wounds she'd observed. *Nah, that only happened in books and movies.*

She picked up her cell. "Tell me you know what this is?"

"No, ma'am, I don't."

She squeezed the phone. *Was she losing it or was Joseph?* He could be someone who refused to accept technology.

Her brother had rejected the simplest tools of the twenty-first century, but he did recognize them. "I'm so tripping."

"Pardon?"

"Never mind. Would you get off me? I need to get to those spectators for help."

"I'm telling you, they aren't there, and you're not running into an open field with lead flying." One eyebrow quirked upward as though his official authority stretched to include her.

She heaved his body mass to the side, rolled to her knees, then rose to both feet. Her head swam. Vertigo, again. When she gained her balance, she ran toward the assembled gathering. Each stride was heavy, the effort to achieve forward momentum seemed unattainable, and she labored for every breath.

Within thirty yards, a strange veil appeared and warbled. Silence substituted the once piercing noise of her surroundings. The inexplicable curtain dissipated, including the crowd. She stopped and strained to locate the spectators, the cars, RV's, anything. Nothing was there. She spun a three-hundred-sixty degree circle. Zero. What the hell just happened?

How did they disappear? Was she frozen in a peculiar window of space and time? Might she be in an atrocious dream from last night's pizza binge with Bethany? She pinched her cheek. "Ouch." *Okay.* She wasn't having a nightmare.

The reverberations from all the weapons resumed. She covered her ears from the transition of silence to the loud overwhelming roar, and the horrifying screams. Scanning the horizon, everything appeared normal, and as far as she could tell, nothing was backward. Most of the soldiers were no longer in well-defined sides, some were charging with their bayonets forward, others were...*Oh, God.* Recipients.

Slowly, she lowered her arms and pivoted, afraid of what she would see next, and the constant reminder there was a distinct possibility she was losing her mind. The usual amount of energy to move returned as well, but the one thing that stood out the most was the smell of death. She gagged. Panic replaced the urge to plead for assistance. She searched for Joseph.

He supported his large frame with one knee on the ground and his right foot ready to take the weight when he stood. The release of the furrowed lines on his forehead revealed he came to some kind of conclusion. His eyes translated worry laced with tenderness and a 'something' she couldn't explain.

A long-winded whistle rented through the awful pandemonium. Joseph rose. "Cheyenne, get down."

Bent at his waist, he ran toward her. His arms gestured to hit the dirt and his gaze changed to trepidation. Terror streaked to each extremity and paralyzed her muscles.

An explosion ripped through the air. The blast's concussion catapulted them several feet from the ground and slammed Joseph back onto the field, then her. "Ugh." Pain shot through her system and her head hurt like hell.

Joseph combat crawled until he was beside her. He wiped her temple with his hand. Blood laced his fingertips. Normally, she would've passed out. Instead, Joseph's soft touch coupled with his caring gaze created an inexplicable calm and tender affection which fluttered from his face to her heart.

Now, she understood why he was a doctor. His comforting contact soothed her ache. She experienced an instantaneous relief from his care. As Joseph swept her hair back, he withdrew a handkerchief from his pocket, bound the laceration and tied a knot.

"How are you?" From his kindhearted gaze, he truly wanted to know.

"Considering what could've happened, I'm fine."

"Can you walk?"

"I think so." She stood, and her legs crumbled.

He scooped her in his powerful arms. "I'll get you back to safety." Joseph's bass voice offered reassurance she desperately needed.

She rested her cheek on his shoulder, and for the few minutes it'd take to return to the field hospital, she gladly let him protect her, his help wouldn't contradict the independence she worked so hard for. She hated to admit it because she didn't know this man, but she liked being in his embrace.

There were so many inexplicable phenomena she experienced within the last hour besides the obvious, like people dematerialized before her eyes and the definite possibility she had face-planted in the nineteenth century specifically, the second of July 1863.

He checked on her every couple of steps and his gaze possessed a gentle yet indefinable emotion.

Although she didn't believe there would be any type of relationship between them, there had been a definite shift inside her soul. No man had ever made a connection to her spirit before.

Deep inside the woods, his pace slowed, and he appeared exhausted. "Joseph?"

"Yes?"

"I can walk from here." She didn't want to relinquish the security of his arms wrapped around her. Everything about him felt right, from his self-confidence to the gentlest touch of any man she had ever known. How odd she would think in idealistic, starry-eyed terms and have notions of an amorous dreamer, when she had better get a grip on reality. Joseph was tired. He carried her due to the fact he was a physician and not because there were any romantic entanglements.

"I'm taking you to my tent so you can rest." He smiled, a hint of deviltry laced the upturned curve of his lips and his to die for emerald eyes twinkled. They reminded her of a light hitting the gorgeous gem while the many faucets of color shimmered and the kind of warm, clear depths she could get lost in. "Then I need to get back to work." His mouth wrinkled.

"I can help." The only way to figure out if she was truly in the nineteenth century was to keep moving and investigate. If she was stuck, then she had better come up with an idea of how to rip the fabric of the damn curtain and get her ass back where she belonged.

She liked technology way too much to be trapped here without her cell phone, computer, car, and her home with an indoor bathroom that included hot water for a shower. Sure, she could find a cosmic pair of scissors to open the partition. "Damn straight I can."

"What?" Joseph slowly released his grip.

She slid down until her feet met the ground and her hip scraped over his groin. He gently grasped her waist and electricity zinged to every cell, even her hair follicles tingled.

Did he feel the same thing? She scrutinized his stare. She trembled from the unbridled fire of desire emanating from his gaze. He drew her into a full frontal embrace, and kissed her.

"Sir?" Twigs crunched behind her.

Joseph's hands visibly shook. He physically placed her in front of him with her back to his chest.

A lanky young man saluted while he wheezed. "Captain Westerly, Lieutenant Rhodes needs you." His head cocked to the side. "Everything okay?"

"Yes, Private. Back to your post. Tell Dr. Rhodes, I'll be there shortly."

"Yes, Sir." The soldier saluted, pivoted and scrambled to follow Joseph's orders.

As soon as he disappeared, she faced Joseph. This handsome man had stolen a piece of her heart, unexplainable but taken.

Chapter Two

"I..." Cheyenne's cheeks changed from an ashen white to the prettiest rose hue Joseph had ever seen as her aquamarine eyes altered like his beloved ocean, from the turbulent waves of a dark green roaring nature's power over man to serenity blue replicating the calm sea he longed for.

"No need to be embarrassed." Joseph drew her into his arms and inhaled. She smelled like a field of blossoming wildflowers. Cheyenne triggered sweet memories of his home situated on a high bluff with the rolling swells of the sea breaking against the rocky shore.

On his property, there was an inlet nestled along the coastline. Westerly Cove had a beautiful beach, trees and a huge boulder perfect for jumping into the ocean. Pangs of longing struck him hard. Joseph didn't realize how much he missed home until Cheyenne reminded him. It had been one hell of a long time since he'd been there. He exhaled.

"That was a big sigh. What are you thinking about?" She upturned her gorgeous face.

"The ocean."

"Which one?" Her eyebrows raised in interest.

"In front of my home." He kissed her pert nose.

"Men and their vague answers. Where?"

He chuckled, enjoying her spunk. Damn, he hadn't laughed in ages, especially since the war had started. She was special, but he understood that when he had first seen her. Cheyenne, he loved her name. "East Coast. Enough about me, where do you hail from?"

"An hour west of here. I drove in to see the reenactment with my girlfriend, Bethany." She whipped a lock of her long raven hair behind her shoulder.

"Reenactment?"

"There's been a lot of…confusion on my part. What's today's date?"

"The second of July."

"What year?" she whispered.

Did she have amnesia? "1863."

"That's what I thought." Her chin lowered.

"Did you come by wagon?" He questioned whether the hit on her head was more serious than he'd first speculated.

Her gaze met his. "No. I came in what's called a car. An automobile." She groaned. "Listen, like it or not, I'm from the twenty-first century. Look." She pointed to her trousers. "These are called blue jeans or pants. This is a zipper and it hasn't been invented yet." *Crap*. She gripped the clasp and tugged. The rasp of metal lasted a few seconds. "I can't believe I stood in front of the Private with my zipper down." The crimson color returned and flushed from her neck to her petite ears.

Hands down, the device was an amazing contraption and he liked how the material bound her luscious ass and encased her toned thighs. He'd never get rid of his hard-on if he continued thinking about her anatomy. *Hard-on?* Not once had he ever used slang when he referred to his cock and how in the hell did he know it was slang?

He couldn't explain the strange sensations, an almost out of the body experience. On numerous occasions many of his patients had confided in him with the threat of death if he mentioned the incident to another person. Now, he understood how they felt.

Was he losing his sanity? He shook his head. Hell, something wasn't right, and the notion had everything to do with meeting this lovely woman. "Cheyenne, I had to hide my erection. Don't worry. I'm sure he didn't notice anything besides a lady wearing undergarments."

"They're not underwear." She stomped her foot.

"Don't stomp your Liverpool plimsolled foot at me."

"Tennis shoes."

"What?"

"Athletic, sneakers. Never mind."

"Listen, you smacked your head pretty hard back there." He looped his arm around hers. "Come, rest in my tent while I tend to the injured." Then he would figure out what in the hell was happening…to both of them. Maybe later, he could ask her more questions and surely by then, he'd be able to find, if not logical, surely suitable explanations.

"I could use some down time, and I doubt if an hour will change my circumstances." She yawned and he fought not to mimic her contagious action, but in the end, he gave in.

Forty-eight hours later, Joseph arched, his spine crackled from top to bottom. A light breeze carried a refreshing reprieve from the horrendous humidity and stench. He peered at the sky. Ominous clouds encroached upon the blue palette. A severe storm was in their future, and he said a quick prayer that the dead would be buried before the downpour. He meandered to the water barrel, stripped down to his trousers and scrubbed the sweat, dirt and the bloody matter off his skin. The last patient required every bit of knowhow and zapped all of his energy. In the end, the brave soldier had passed.

What started out as minor skirmishes expanded into three days of unspeakable bloodshed. Twenty-four hours ago, the last shot was fired, and the makeshift hospital had been inundated with soldiers from both sides. Although he didn't know the exact count, the amount of casualties boggled his mind even as an experienced veteran.

Finally, the flow of the injured had subsided, and God bless the civilians from the town and countryside who volunteered to help care for the men and bury the dead. Tending the wounded would continue, but the new enemy was infections, somehow he understood about the tiny microorganisms.

He'd told his fellow physicians and surgeons, but they'd laughed, except for Lieutenant Rhodes. Aggressive and vicious, germs turned soldier's extremities to gangrene which was why amputations were considered merciful. If the soldiers were lucky enough to survive, there was a ton of other things vying to kill them. He scanned the crowded grounds of the field hospital; the men lay virtually on top of each other. He shook his head in disgust and said a quick prayer.

"Captain Westerly, I don't know about you, but I'm exhausted." Lieutenant Rhodes stretched his back. The rippled pop of each vertebrae echoed like his did earlier.

"Joseph. After what we've been through, I think we can dispense with formalities, William."

"Wonder who won?"

"If there was any gain whatsoever, I can't begin to fathom which side accomplished the most. By the way, you did a fine job. I'm impressed you diagnosed and treated injuries even a seasoned surgeon would've missed." Joseph grabbed a towel and dabbed the droplets trickling down his chest from the sponge bath.

"Thanks. I've been thinking."

"Hmm." He lifted his chin for the young doctor to continue.

"I talked to a fearless gentleman by the name of Custer. They raised his rank again to a Brigadier General of volunteers. I want to join the rather unorthodox chap. I could be part of something extraordinary. Like...saving lives while seeing the states and possibly the territories, serving our country and my name being remembered, written down as part of our history. Does that sound arrogant?"

"No, not at all, but you furnished a list of reasons for justifying your ambition. I'm going to ask one question only you can answer. Is that really what you want to do? If the answer is yes, then it doesn't matter what I, or anyone else thinks. As your senior officer, I can put in a request although, I can't guarantee anything."

"Thank you, Sir." William smiled. "I can't tell you what your intercession means. Besides the adventure, I could learn a lot. Do you think they'll take me because of my size? I'm taller and larger than most cavalrymen?"

"You'll find out soon enough." Joseph finger combed his wet hair.

"Captain Westerly and Lieutenant Rhodes, I have a message." The private handed him a missive.

"Thanks." Joseph read the note. "William, you are to report to the evacuation site and leave with the wagons and tend the injured. I'm to stay here for a few days."

"Yes, Sir." William saluted, then departed.

"Private, meet me outside my tent in five minutes. I have a petition I want you to deliver." Joseph buttoned his shirt and slid his suspenders in place.

"Yes, Sir."

As Joseph plodded toward his temporary quarters, he recalled Cheyenne had risen on several occasions. Her gaze searched the battlefield near the tree where they met, and her forehead wrinkled as if looking for answers none of them had. Her shoulders slumped, and she returned to his tent with a disillusioned gaze, which tore him apart. He felt helpless and a bit strange.

There was a connection to this lovely lady. A

premonition surfaced, did their bond stem from a past encounter or a previous carnal knowledge? He admitted, from the depths of his soul, he had met her before. For some reason, he couldn't begin to fathom, he had accepted she was from the twenty-first century, so how could he have met her?

Had the future collapsed into the present? When he was a young lad, these were the same topics raised with his private tutor. He had ridiculed his teacher for believing in such nonsense. He silenced the nagging thoughts, and after folding the request he'd finished, he handed it to the private. "Thanks. Take care of yourself."

"Yes, Sir." The private cleared his throat. "There's a Miss Johnson waiting to see you."

"Tell her, I'll be right out." Joseph remained until the young man exited, then pivoted and ambled to the adjoining tent. He flipped the first flap to the side, then the second and strode over to the pallet.

Cheyenne slept peacefully. He gingerly removed the kerchief and brushed her straight, black hair to the side. The wound was clean and healing nicely.

He bent over, kissed her button nose, realizing he loved it. Loved? How strange he had employed the sentiment again. She bewitched him in every sense. He smoothed and tucked the blanket around her frame. "Sleep well, my Indian Princess."

He'd better see what Miss Johnson wanted; no doubt his services were needed. He stepped outside. "Miss Johnson, how can I help you today?"

"There was a skirmish at Mrs. Dibello's farm.

Our soldiers are wounded. I think the fighting scared the poor woman into labor and I was told you were knowledgeable with birthing complications. Would you please see to our men as well as help with Mrs. Dibello?" Miss Johnson batted her eyelashes one too many times.

"I'll handle the soldiers, but don't you have a town physician or midwife?"

"Our only doctor is with a regiment down Virginia way and Mable's drunk."

"Where is the farm?" Joseph intended to talk with his commanding officer and obtain permission to see to the injured and Mrs. Dibello.

"Head north about thirty minutes until you reach the spring fed lake, then go east for twenty. Here is a horse you can use. His name is Rocket." She offered the reins. "I'll help here until the injured are transported."

He gripped the leather leads she offered and ground tethered them. "I'll grab my bags and if there are any problems, I'll let you know. Don't worry about Mrs. Dibello, she'll be fine."

"Thank you." Miss Johnson clutched his arm and brazenly tightened her grip. "I appreciate everything you've done for the Union cause."

"I don't pay much attention to which side these men pay their allegiance to, Miss Johnson. I have both under my watch. These soldiers are human beings and need my care. Now, kindly release me." He swallowed the animosity and several doses of repugnance for this woman. The tongue lashing he wanted to give to her wouldn't do a damn bit of good.

"You're not bitter the Rebels have killed our boys?"

"No, Miss Johnson, I'm not." Her heart had been hardened by death and brutalized by this cursed war. Those type of wounds were not visible and hard as hell to recover from.

"I guess I should be ashamed." She freed him and lowered her chin.

"Death doesn't select sides, men do. And whether you are Union or Confederate, the passing of any loved one hurts. We should choose compassion over hostility and empathy verses hatred. What say you?"

"If my mother had lived, she would be mortified of my behavior. It's been hard. I'm the eldest now and responsible for my siblings. Eight in all. All of my older brothers have fallen and I haven't heard from my pop in over a year. How will I make it?" Tears streamed down her cheeks.

He withdrew a handkerchief from his pocket and offered the cloth to the distraught woman. "Don't fret. Things have a way of working out. Let me see what I can do. But promise me one thing?"

She nodded and grasped the hankie.

"Treat each one of these soldiers as if they were your father or brothers, and before long, your soul will mend."

Her head bobbed a couple of times; she wiped the moisture from her face with the hankie he had given to her, turned and walked away.

"Miss Johnson?"

She halted.

"What is your dad's name?"

Miss Johnson spun. Her face brightened, and the beginning of a smile tugged at each end of her mouth. "Benjamin."

"I'll see what I can find out."

"Thank you." She whirled, and there was a skip in her walk as she proceeded toward the ambulances, the two and four-wheeled wagons used as transports.

"That was very sweet of you." He pivoted on the ball of his foot and met Cheyenne's gaze filled with what appeared to be admiration.

If he had been the blushing sort which he wasn't, he'd have done so by now. "I don't deserve your esteem. Any man worth his salt would've done the same thing."

"Well I do declare Captain Joseph Westerly, you're embarrassed. The tips of your ears are a dead giveaway."

"My ears are not red." Dammit all the way to hell, he sensed the heat spreading. "What is the southern accent about?" He changed the subject.

"Er, um, I was mimicking a character from a book, then it was made into a movie."

"Movie?"

"Moving still pictures. I'm thinking it'll be invented around 1895." She scratched her head as though trying to remember a fact he wasn't sure was one. He couldn't explain why, but there was a certain credence he afforded to Cheyenne. Had it been anyone else, he would have had one retort, balderdash.

"You're a wealth of information. How about you come with me and we will discuss more of these moving pictures?"

"I don't know if I should leave." She glanced at their tree once more. "But...I don't know how to get back."

"I've been thinking. If there is a portal, your best chance may be next week."

"When?" Puzzlement mixed with apprehension spanned across her face.

"The Irish Brigade fought today. Strange as it may sound, consider this...In keeping with Celtic beliefs, your journey through the different worlds could happen on the next Gaelic phase."

"The what?"

"Moon phase. The full moon was on Tuesday and is now waning. Count 'em, four more days."

"Oh, puh-leeease."

"You have any other ideas?"

Her forehead scrunched. The linear lines deepened. "What are my options?" She paced the length of the tent and back. "I'm not sure if I have any other choices?" Cheyenne pivoted, resumed her steps along the same path, rotated, and returned. When she halted in front of him, resignation transpired into an unreadable expression. "If I can't get home..." Her voice had lowered to a whisper. "How will I survive this era?" Cheyenne's lips quivered, and she visibly shook.

He wrapped his arms around her and understood Cheyenne's indecipherable countenance from a moment ago was pure trepidation. "I won't leave you. You can stay or as the circumstances are now, go with me." He wasn't sure why he gave a damn, but he did. How had this woman burrowed under his skin and found a home in his heart? She may not know it yet, but his Indian Princess had a part of his soul too.

"Give me a minute." She snuggled against his chest.

"Take whatever you need. I'm right here." Although soldiers were in dire straits and required his expertise, there were other traumas he refused to disregard. Cheyenne needed him, and he'd be there. She was frightened, but she had inner strength. How in the hell did he know that? His muscles tensed.

The knowledge she coexisted within his spirit startled him and at the same time, was empowering. He couldn't rationalize the sensations and interpreting the phenomena was futile. He discerned Cheyenne's soul comingled with his which generated an understanding of her internal fortitude and her weaknesses. The vast implications boggled his logical mind.

"Where are we headed?" She released him, withdrew several inches and a steadfast determination radiated from her gaze.

"Mrs. Dibello's farm." He swept the flaps from the tent to the side, strode inside, then snatched his saddle bags from the floor. His steps were lighter knowing his Indian Princess was going with him.

"I should warn you. I um, I don't do blood well."

"I'm sure there are a million other things you could do for me or Mrs. Dibello besides fainting." He brushed her hair behind one ear and kissed her cheek. "Don't worry, under the proviso you do, I'll be there to catch you."

"Yeah right. I'm so screwed."

He chuckled. He loved her expressions and gazed into her enchanting eyes. What else would he discover about Cheyenne and fall in love with? He suppressed the last thought. Although lately, when it came to Cheyenne, he was thinking in those terms a great deal, and the idea wasn't as awful as it had been in his past. Any other time, when a woman eyed him as husband material, he high-tailed it the other way, but his Indian Princess wasn't thinking about him along those lines, he was. "On our way out, I need to do a few things."

Chapter Three

Cheyenne climbed on a rock, clasped Joseph's forearm and lifted her leg over the horse's back. She landed on the blanket in front of him and gripped the withers. Her wrists rested on the medical saddle bags hung over the dun's shoulders while she adjusted her knees around them.

"Did you get Miss Johnson taken care of?" She fidgeted gaining a better balance.

"Everything worked out well. Lieutenant Rhodes orders have been postponed for several days and the young private volunteered to help with Miss Johnson's work load. It seems Charles is familiar with the mechanisms of a farm."

"That's great, but I can't get comfy." She glanced over her shoulder and a pained facial countenance met her. "You okay?"

"Are you finished wiggling?"

"Sorry. But I feel like the stallion's backbone is going to split me in two."

"Lean against me." He gently guided her back to rest against his chest. "That help?"

"Ah, what a difference." Then she understood why his face contorted in agony. His hard-on rubbed her rear. "I could ride behind you." *Or on you since we have an automatic rocker.* She smiled.

"Not a chance in hell." His lips turned upward, and his grin extended to his eyes. He snaked his arms through hers and lightly grasped the reins. She latched onto the crook of his elbows and held tight.

He clicked his tongue. Rocket pranced sideways for several yards, before he charged forward. Joseph swayed with the mount's graceful canter as though he was one with the horse. The steed galloped across the open pasture and the fresh air whisked by, whipping her hair in every direction. She glimpsed at the elastic band on her wrist, a lot of good the colorful accessory was doing there. Oh bother, she didn't care. She was glad to leave the acrid smells of war and death behind. With Joseph, she remained safe, and she chose to enjoy the journey and the scenery.

She tilted her chin several inches in the air and gazed at the turbulent clouds stirring in the gray sky. The birds floated and circled on the aloft winds. The temperature had cooled considerably from yesterday's heat and humidity. With Joseph's upper torso enveloping hers, his body transferred the warmth she needed. In every instance, he had taken care of her, and with that lovely thought, she burrowed further into the cocoon he offered.

Joseph lightly drew on the leather reins. When Rocket slowed to a trot, Joseph offered praises for a job well done. "Magnificent animal, I'm surprised he hasn't been conscripted."

Her butt thumped with each stride. "Uh, can Rocket walk?"

"Of course, he can."

"Then do it." She clenched her teeth together

until the beast under them leisurely reduced his speed. "My molars thank you, but I bit my tongue."

"I think I need to look at your wound."

She angled her head toward him and stuck out her tongue.

His lips separated, and he swooped. The flavor of mint burst across her taste buds, as he examined every inch of her mouth. Cheyenne's pulse pounded, and her temperature rose with every luscious stroke of Joseph's crusade to assess her injury. He was a potent healer, she didn't hurt anymore, but now her breasts ached. She craved Joseph's touch. She wanted him to lave her nipples, then suckle, but he seemed intent on restoring her tongue back to health.

She inhaled through her nose. He smelled like the powerful stallion beneath them, the great outdoors, and all male. Her heart skipped a beat then drummed a steady song, solely for Joseph. How had one man captured her senses and possessed her soul in forty-eight hours? Something Cheyenne had promised she wouldn't allow again.

Joseph released her, and his tender gaze spoke volumes. He brushed the back of his fingers against her cheek and sighed. "It shouldn't be much longer. We should make it to Mrs. Dibello's before it rains."

Her heart palpitated because she desired his caress, and she missed his contact which scared her also. She vowed never to let a man close again, something she had promised years ago. Doug had manipulated her mental state until her emotional well-being died. Her best friend, Bethany, urged her to see a therapist.

After she sought help, her ex-fiancé had laughed. He called her every lowlife name she heard before and some she hadn't. Since then, she refused to let any guy get close, because she didn't want to be vulnerable again.

He nudged her back into the crook of his arm, and his thumb lifted her chin. "You're miles away. Your expressive eyes expose your hurt, and your taut muscles tell me you're frightened." He kissed her nose. "What's going on in your pretty head?" His whispered words conveyed he earnestly wanted to know.

Or would his true colors emerge after she'd been sucked into another poisoned relationship? "Are you being the kind doctor or simply bored?"

He tensed for a long moment, then expelled a lengthy breath. "Clearly, I've offended you. My sincere apologies."

"I'm sorry." She patted the top of his hand and chose to be forthright. "I haven't known you for very long."

"True."

"Yet, I've let you in here." She rested her palm over her heart.

"Is that so?"

"Yeah." She straightened her spine.

"Daunting isn't it?"

"Yes." Cheyenne realized if Joseph asked, she'd share her deepest secrets. How could a special bond transpire so quickly? She needed to get a grip on reality. Joseph was here merely to protect her until she returned to the twenty-first century. Was she unconsciously seeking a relationship?

She exhaled a long breath and admitted she had admiration and affection for Joseph with an extra-large dose of intense desire. Would she call it love at first sight? When she first met Joseph, she didn't particularly like him, but something extraordinary percolated inside her. She sucked in a lung full of air, maybe Joseph was her soul mate.

Her chest involuntarily squeezed. She had better keep her emotions in check. Joseph had a life here, and her home was a hundred and fifty years in the future. Even assuming they fell in love, comingling their lives would prove impossible. Joseph couldn't practice in the twenty-first century. Under the condition she was unable to leave, she'd miss the technology, but what scared her the most, would she be able to subsist? If she left…

A small niggle reminded her, she did have feelings for Joseph, and there was a distinct possibility grief was in her future. She dispelled the sad thought and chose to believe there was a positive reason for this to happen. Besides, she was getting way ahead of herself. "Can I get off just for a minute? My butt is sore. I'm not used to riding."

"Sure. This is a perfect place beside the lake. We can take cover in those trees over there." He lightly drew the reins, and Rocket halted.

She slid off, and strode to the edge of the woods, ducked under a couple of limbs, and leaned against the trunk of a large tree. Joseph watered Rocket, and led him beneath the green canopy, then ground tethered him.

Joseph stepped through the knee high grass and

mimicked her position. "Smells like rain."

The humidity packed the air almost to the saturation point. She inhaled, and the moisture filled her lungs. "I love summer showers."

"Looks like we'll get one." Joseph pivoted slightly. His fingers caressed her jawline and stopped at her mouth. He had the softest touch, loving, and caring. He lifted her chin as his gaze secured hers, his desire inundated her senses.

She caressed his right cheek, the shadow of his light beard grazed her palm, and she licked her lips, wanting him in every conceivable way possible. He closed the distance between them, acknowledging her silent request.

Under the spell of frantic need, she met him halfway, and devoured his lips, craving his attention. Joseph gripped the back of her head, and with the same determination, opened his mouth, accepted her tongue, then thrust forward with his. The duel of eager enthusiasm ratcheted her passion. She circled his neck with one hand while the other skimmed the edge of his suspenders to his waist, and slipped further down. She cupped his balls, then stroked the length of his cock.

He growled, as her palms curved to his ass, and added pressure until her pelvic bone touched his engorged cock. Her hips undulated. She enjoyed the raging lust surging through her veins. She never did this with a guy she had just met, but the mysterious enticement was beyond her wildest fantasies. His hands mimicked hers, squeezed each of her butt cheeks and lifted her frame. He changed her circular motion to up and down.

"This won't do." He positioned her back against the trunk while his fingertips unsnapped the top button of her jeans. As he tugged the fabric, the sound of her zipper filled the air and he stilled.

"Don't you dare stop." She caught his wrist and applied the pressure for the release she needed, no, craved from this man she had connected with only a few days ago, but felt like she'd known forever. She couldn't explain why she hungered for his intimate touch, and sought to fill the emptiness.

"I meant to look at that fancy contraption…but, later." Joseph hungrily kissed her lips and his tongue delved into her mouth while his fingertips found her clit and pinched. Blinded by aroused ecstasy, she closed her eyes. One of his fingers slipped inside her channel, and as he flexed each joint, she ground against his palm, enjoying the intimacy and warmth.

She grappled to open his placket. After what she deemed an eternity, she abandoned her campaign, and palmed his hard shaft. The size lured her imagination further from reality. Stunned at her next erotic desire, she gasped. She wanted him inside and to surround the length and breadth of his cock. She quivered from the euphoric high her fantasies inspired, her utopia.

When he freed her lips from his potent kiss, his mouth lowered to her neck and suckled. He definitely demonstrated the fine points of foreplay.

"Ahh." She found his ear, followed the swirl down to the lobe and scored his skin with her teeth.

"My sweet Indian Princess, it's time." He abandoned his crusade, then wreaked havoc on her clit. With one swift counter rotation, she launched, fireworks exploded like the Fourth of July finale. The phosphorescent colors rained down until the beautiful sparkles diminished.

He loosened his grasp. She slid down the tree, intoxicated from the bliss he delivered. Joseph snagged her arms before her rear hit the ground. He lifted her into a heartfelt hug, one she wouldn't forget as long as she lived. When her legs had gained their strength, she stood on her own.

Far too quickly, he added space between them. "Open your beautiful eyes so I can see my magnificent sea."

When she did, his gaze imparted sorrow. "You're sad. Do you miss it?"

"Not anymore." Joseph closed the distance. The back of his fingers cascaded over her cheek and ended at her chin. His thumb traced the bottom line of her lip until Joseph's mouth reunited with hers.

The tender devotion he bequeathed was like a prayer to a saint, hallowed, revered, and she'd add, an incredible mind-blowing experience. Her arms circled his neck while her hands twirled his blond hair. A chain twisted around her finger. "Sorry." She untangled the necklace.

"No harm done." His tongue frolicked from her mouth and skimmed to the sensitive skin behind her ear. As her shoulder curled, he chuckled, then drifted toward the front of her neck. His finger hooked on the V of her T-shirt and lowered the material.

He jerked backward, astonishment flashed across his gaze. "A corset substitute. I've heard about them, but I've never seen one."

"It's called a brassiere. A bra. Do you like what you see?" She crossed her fingers, the lacey push-up number cost her a pretty penny. There were a lot of things she couldn't explain the past couple of days, including her affection for this man, and she added one more. His opinion mattered.

"I like what's inside the...bra, better." Joseph carefully withdrew her breasts and held one in each hand as his gaze revealed a reverence. "Beautiful."

Delighted he was pleased, she smiled. Joseph was different than any other man she'd met. It figured she had to travel a hundred-fifty plus years to find him.

Joseph's teeth scraped over the tip of her breast.

"Ah."

"You like that?"

"Uh-huh." Fog filled her brain. Words were not traveling the proper channel to her mouth. The murky haze combined with the exhilarating sensations surging throughout her system meant her paradise was around the corner and several paces away.

He sucked ravenously. His middle finger slid inside her core while his palm massaged her clit and applied perfect pressure.

She recanted, make that one step. "Joseph?"

"Hmm." His tongue swathed a path across her areola.

She fisted his hair and screamed, pure ecstasy captured her soul.

When she returned from her rapture, Joseph

righted her clothing. "I could stay here all day with you, but we need to get going."

"What about you?"

"Nothing would thrill me more, but I have duties."

"Not even." Her hands seized each hip and halted his movement. She gazed into his narrowed glare, lowered to her knees, then unbuttoned the front placket of his trousers. Joseph's breath hitched, and his pupils dilated, constricting his beautiful irises. As much as she adored Joseph's emerald eyes, his look of lust generated an intense desire to grant his wish, but the size of his cock intimidated her.

She gently grasped the root of his shaft and squeezed. His male essence beaded on the crown, and she swirled her tongue over the head, tasting the masculine pearl. The musky spice burst across her taste buds. "Hmm." The involuntary response surged from her throat, negating the fear she had earlier. She opened her mouth and welcomed Joseph's cock.

His hands cupped the back of her head, and he selected a genteel rhythm. Her gaze journeyed to Joseph's clenched jaw and a muscle ticked. He didn't want to lose control and hurt her? Well, she had other plans.

She picked up the pace, and with one hand, she lightly compressed his balls. He groaned, and closed his eyes. Bingo. When he released his jaw and panted, finally enjoying their union, she felt like it was Christmas in July, and she wanted to sing a hallelujah chorus. Crazy as it sounded, she heard the music inside her head.

With every piston of his hips, she sucked, savoring his juices. Once Joseph freed the shackles of his anxieties, his cadence increased, and his shaft bumped the back of her mouth. Thrilled by unhampered concerns, her other hand followed each stroked of her lips. He quickened his tempo.

"God, Cheyenne, you're magnificent. It's time." He began to pull away.

"Nuh-uh." As she continued to glide the length of his shaft.

"My sweet Indian Princess." His head tilted back and a satisfied moan filled their lush sanctuary. As he came, his creamy seed spurted, and she swallowed, satiating her thirst. She licked the remnants from his cock and gradually released him. She carefully buttoned his pants and wondered if they would ever have a chance for an encore. He helped her rise, and from his gaze, his emerald gems shimmered with what seemed to be admiration.

"You're magnificent." His palms embraced each cheek of her face, and he lowered his head, whispering kisses across her lips until she opened her mouth. He accepted her invitation and kissed her. Their wonderful union opened her heart further to receive Joseph's undivided love and attention.

****

With Joseph's help, Cheyenne dismounted from Rocket, and the clouds erupted into a torrential downpour. "Get Mrs. Dibello's barn door." Lightning struck nearby, and she barely heard him over the clap of thunder.

She ran to the outbuilding, lifted the two-by-four from its cradle, threw one door to the side, then the other. Without any prodding from Joseph, Rocket strutted inside. She closed the both entrances and secured them. Chilled to the bone, she picked at her clothing stuck to her skin.

Joseph slid off of Rocket to the dirt floor and the horse nickered, nudging his arm. He assigned the stallion a stall, wiped him down with a fistful of hay, and gave him fresh water.

Groans from the loft overcame the deluge of raindrops hitting the roof. "While I examine the men, would you go to the house and assess Mrs. Dibello?"

"Assess? You've got to be kidding me. Don't you remember? Band-Aid, faint, congruous—"

"Mrs. Dibello will tell you what I need to know." He hefted the saddle bags over his shoulder, hustled up the ladder and climbed onto the second level, ignoring her smartass comment while bits of seed and dust floated to the ground.

Surely, establishing Mrs. Dibello's status should be easy, she pivoted, removed the horse blanket off the top rail, and held it over her head, then sprinted to the house dodging puddles. The cabin door was open so she knocked on the threshold. Water dripped from her clothing and pooled on the wooden porch. She shook out Rocket's cover, laid it over the railing, bound her wet tresses with the elastic band and tucked the ends.

"Howdy." A wide-eyed young girl greeted her with a smidgeon of trepidation.

"My name is Cheyenne. What's yours?" She opted to ease the child's uneasiness and squatted.

"Elizabeth." Her big baby-blues twinkled, revealing her fear had vanished.

"Doctor Westerly is in the barn, and I've come to see Mrs. Dibello. Is she your mom?"

"Yes, ma'am." Elizabeth captured her hand and tugged. "Hurry, she's in a bad way."

Cheyenne lurched to her feet, trailed Elizabeth, and hoped the youngster exaggerated her mother's condition. The smell of homemade stew and biscuits permeated the air. They marched around a rectangular table laden with leftovers from several meals. Their kitchen nestled along the right wall included an indoor pump, stacked dirty dishes in the sink waiting to be washed, and steam rose from a pot on an old time stove. On the opposite side were two open doorways. Elizabeth hauled her through the first one.

"Oh my God." Cheyenne silently mouthed the words.

"Please save my baby." Mrs. Dibello's sweat-ridden hair clung to her ashen face.

"Joseph, I mean, Dr. Westerly, is in the barn…" Cheyenne swallowed hard. "Tell me what to do and I'll try and help."

"Elizabeth, go do your chores." Mrs. Dibello spoke through clenched teeth.

"I don't have any."

"Go."

Elizabeth bugged out of the room and closed the door.

"Look and see why the baby is stuck." She

clutched her stomach and whimpered.

Cheyenne bit her bottom lip and lifted the quilt. Dizzy, she inhaled, chastising her weakness. *Get it together. This family is depending on you and so is the baby.*

Chapter Four

The soldiers had settled for the night. Joseph stretched his spine. His lower back muscles ached from bending over. In a few minutes, he would be fine. His worst patient coughed, twisted and turned from the pain. Afraid the movement would tear the stitches he'd meticulously sewn, he checked the bandages and dripped some laudanum between his lips. Soon, he fell into a peaceful sleep. The men needed all the rest they could, because Lieutenant Rhodes promised several wagons would be sent first thing in the morning, and by his internal clock, he guessed the sun would be rising shortly.

Joseph climbed down the ladder and found two water buckets and washed from one of them. The soldiers had insisted he should take care of the woman and the babe coming into the world first, but he assured them Mrs. Dibello was in capable hands. If things progressed where Cheyenne needed his assistance, she would've summoned him. Once he had repeated his reassurances, they relaxed. However, it was strange Cheyenne hadn't returned to the barn. He figured she would've been begging for his help.

He tossed the saddle bags over his shoulder, grabbed the last clean pail of water and headed for the house. The rain had stopped, and the dawn's light of muted pinks and blues had broken the eastern sky. He dodged the runoff, mud puddles and tiptoed through the mire coagulating into sludge. When he reached the bottom step of the porch, he rinsed off his boots, then climbed the balance. At the threshold, a groggy little girl greeted him.

"Are you the doctor?" She fisted her hands and rubbed her eyes.

"Dr. Westerly at your service." He smiled, trying not to scare the tyke. He probably looked like a convict rather than a refined gentleman, who loved to waltz and was told when he danced, he had light feet. He enjoyed the sway of each step and the music. Those memories seemed eons ago, and he doubted if he'd ever get the chance to dance with Cheyenne. He had to constantly remind himself that soon, she would be gone.

"My name is Elizabeth. They're in that room." She pointed.

He strode into where Elizabeth aimed her finger, and closed the door behind him with a little apprehension over what he'd find. He scanned the small space. On one side of the bedroom, soiled sheets and blankets were piled waist high on the wooden floor next to Mrs. Dibello's cleaned bed. The new mother was washed and well-groomed for what she'd been through and slept.

To the right, a soft glow emanated from an oil lantern perched on the fireplace mantel. Cheyenne rocked the infant in a steady rhythm while the hand woven rug underneath quieted the sound. Her gaze met his.

"We did it." She stage whispered through a grin, and her eyes sparkled. "Come meet Andrew." A special light emanated from her eyes after the remarkable occasion of bringing a baby into the world. He always experienced it too and was happy for Cheyenne.

He crossed the room, lifted Andrew wrapped in a quilt onto one arm, and checked his body temperature. He chuckled when the newborn wiggled under his palm.

The sound of horses and wagons clamored outside. "Sounds like they're here to pick up the wounded. While I check on Mrs. Dibello and this little fellow, why don't you go see if anyone needs help?" He placed the baby beside his mom. "Cheyenne, thanks for all you're doing. I'm proud of you."

He surreptitiously viewed Cheyenne rise. She strode across the space, opened the door and paused without turning around. "Mrs. Dibello's a nurse. She knew what to do, coached me through every single stage. I don't know how she did it. I had to stitch...I didn't think I could do—"

"When I had my first patient, I thought the same thing. What your feeling is normal. You allowed me the time to care for the men. They aren't more important, but they are someone's family."

She turned and faced him. "Her husband was killed. How can these women take all this crap life is handing them? It's wrong."

Mrs. Dibello snuggled Andrew to her side.

He strode over to Cheyenne, placed both hands

on her waist and drew her into his embrace. He hovered above Cheyenne's ear, whispering in the softest tone he could muster. "No one can confidently say that he will still be living tomorrow."

"Euripides." Cheyenne hugged him.

"I don't have any answers. Life gives, then takes. This I do understand, it's how you live through it that's important. Today, you have saved two souls, be happy." He kissed her cheek. "I promise to give Mrs. Dibello a thorough examination, but I'll bet a gold piece you did an outstanding job."

Cheyenne released him. "Mrs. Dibello is one hell of a woman." She pivoted and disappeared from his sight.

When Cheyenne fled the room, she carried with her the most important part of him, his heart. The realization he had to let Cheyenne go back to her family and friends gutted him. Maybe, he could talk her into staying, to be his wife and to have his children. Who was he kidding; he wasn't ready to settle down. The war raged with no end in sight, and he considered his death a probable outcome.

"Doctor?" Mrs. Dibello's voice sounded strong.

"I'm right here." He closed the door.

By the time he finished his examination, served the stew and biscuits kept warm on the stove to Mrs. Dibello and Elizabeth, the kitchen had been cleaned spotless, and the wagons had long since departed. With Mrs. Dibello's blessing, he ladled two more bowls and proceeded to the barn. He located Cheyenne asleep in one of the stalls with a blanket draped over the top of fresh hay.

Setting the plates on a wooden tack box in the breeze way, the hollow echo meant Mrs. Dibello had to sell the equipment for food or the army conscripted the gear. He shook his head, pondering the same question Cheyenne had asked him earlier. *How will these folks make it? Not only Mrs. Dibello, Elizabeth, and Miss Johnson, but the scores of soldiers and young boys too.*

He lay beside Cheyenne, wanting to make love to her and forget about this crazy world. The back of his hand met Cheyenne's cheek. His lips followed suit, skimming down to her jaw, tracking the contour. She awakened, and the desire in her gaze confirmed she craved him also. Her palms clasped each side of his face, and her mouth eagerly sought his. He accepted what she graciously offered and explored.

She shadowed his crusade. Her hands drifted to his shoulders, she slid off his suspenders and unbuttoned his shirt. He'd given his undershirt to a sick soldier long ago during an especially harsh winter storm, and the man had lived. The gentleman promised when the war was over, and when he could, he'd pay him back in kind. It was doubtful, but Joseph was glad to help.

Her fingertips kneaded his chest, and her touch scorched his flesh. His heart rate increased, each temple throbbed in unison, thudding a tune meant for one thing. He'd have the sweetest release with this beautiful lady. Her campaign journeyed down to his randy cock. She stroked the full length several times before he stopped her attention. He seized control. It was his turn to give her pleasure.

He removed her soft cotton blouse. The newfangled brassiere was sheer, wholly feminine, and his cock pulsed. She rolled over and he unfastened the bra, then she flipped to her back. Her beautiful breasts beckoned for his devotion. His mouth encased her rose nipple as his tongue swept across the areola. She arched seeking more. He chuckled. She was appreciative, responsive, and exclusively his to love. His balls burned for relief, and his cock begged to be inside this incredible woman, to feel her tight channel and moist heat.

****

When Cheyenne curved her spine for more of Joseph's devotion and he'd chuckled deep within his lungs, her hips involuntarily mimicked every exploit of his mouth. The electricity surging through her system increased exponentially with each swath of his wonderful tongue. Her hand delved to his rigid silken shaft and stroked from the base to the tip. With her thumb, she rubbed the bead of moisture across the top.

He groaned and released her breast. His mouth wandered to her waist. Within seconds, he stripped her jeans off. His hungry gaze fell on her lace covered panties, and she was glad she had worn her sexy pair rather than some of her dilapidated ones. She wanted to appear sensual, erotic even. Joseph's opinion counted, and from his gaze, she had scored several points.

His index finger trailed the elastic perimeter of her panties from one side to the other, snagged the seam and dragged the fabric several inches downward. She lifted her hips, and the material slid with ease until he divested her of the barrier. Still at her feet, Joseph's ravenous gaze landed on her bared feminine folds.

When she had been with her ex-fiancé, she'd wait for his next move. Doug demanded her submission, and normally, he'd get off and leave her wanting. Cheyenne understood Joseph was different in every way.

Feeling decadent, she widened her knees, her hands skimmed to her pussy, and she spread her feminine lips.

Joseph moaned. "So lovely." His ragged voice thrilled her.

He kissed her toes, traveled up her legs until he covered the bundle of nerves with his mouth. When he'd taken two laves across her clit, she gripped a handful of his hair. She bucked and held on for the ride of her life. His mouth journeyed to her opening; he thrust his tongue inside, emulating what she hoped his cock would be doing next. His finger replaced his tongue, and his mouth found purchase on her clit. Guess he had other plans. Her orgasm was so close, she rocked against his face. Joseph repositioned his hand, dipped two fingers and his thumb into her moisture. His middle finger circled the tight ring of her anus and slid into her dark channel, while the other slipped inside her core. His thumb rubbed her clit. He massaged her bud and curled his fingers. Her hips pumped under his lethal spell, her release imminent.

His other hand found her breast and his thumb and forefinger tweaked her nipple.

"Joseph?"

"Go my Indian Princess." He applied pressure on her clit and pinched her nipple again.

She launched into the stratosphere and flew beyond to a beautiful boundary where heaven and earth met. With the world below, she floated through the air, until she landed, sated, and happy. There really was a heaven on earth.

His loving ministrations continued, and she opened her eyes. He gradually concluded his considerations and let go. He nibbled on her belly, then he sat on his ankles between her legs.

"Enjoyed it did you?" A grin plastered across his handsome face.

"You know I did." Now that she wasn't in the throes of passion, she tried for indiscretion and tightened her knees against his side.

"Oh no, you don't." His elbows widened her again. "I love looking at you. You're perfect in every sense of the word."

Her core swelled. His palm trailed his ravenous gaze and feasted on her expanded clit.

"Beautiful." His fingers entered her channel, and while he fingered her, he extended his legs. He lingered above her pussy. "Exquisite." His moist breath feathered across her vulva. He lowered his mouth and captured her bud, then massaged the pearl. Within several of his loving strokes, she was beyond ready.

"Joooo," she crooned, wanting his cock inside her.

He rose slightly from her and smiled. With predatory eyes and the supremacy of an alpha male, he crawled the length of her. In one swift thrust, he filled her. Slowly, he advanced, then retreated, as his mouth found one of her nipples and suckled. She undulated beneath his massive frame, loving every drive of his hard cock, and the devotion he gave to her breast.

After sucking, his teeth scraped across the peak, then his tongue laved. He alternated never using the same sequence. His attention to detail heightened the sensual sensations traveling through her body at the speed of light, eliciting an erotic expanse of electric scintillations.

Just like her special recipe of Chai tea she had formulated, the unique blend of aphrodisiacs ensured the arousal of sexual desire and amplification of passion, especially in men. Joseph created the same spectacular cocktail solely for her enjoyment.

He released her nipple, both of Joseph's palms slid under her rear and lifted. With her hips off the ground, he selected a slow rhythm. As the intensity escalated, his pace increased. His thick cock coupled with Joseph's raw power and his fervor focused on her pleasure, he propelled her to the verge of her orgasm.

Her hand journeyed to his balls, and she gently grasped them. He inhaled a colossal breath, thrust two more times, and the veins in his throat bulged. When he expelled the air along with his essence, she joined him. Explosions of ecstasy detonated, and she called for more.

He lowered her hips, laid beside her and nuzzled her neck. "I'd love to, but I'm going to need some time." His throaty laugh dragged her back to the present.

"I said that out loud?"

"More like demanded." He swept her long tresses behind her ear and whispered, "I assure you, I intend to fulfill every wish and fantasy you harbor."

Excitement barreled through her system, and her skin pebbled in anticipation. "See that you do."

"Are you hungry? I have some of Mrs. Dibello's stew."

"Famished."

Joseph rose, and he shuffled on his pants sans shirt while she scurried into her clothing. She dipped the crusty bread into the concoction and nibbled. "Yum." Even though the food was tepid, she wolfed down the mixture. She hadn't eaten since breakfast on the morning of the reenactment. For two and a half days they ate the munchies she had brought. After finishing the scrumptious blend of meat and vegetables, she observed Joseph. He appeared to be a thousand miles away.

"A penny for your thoughts."

He never answered her. Joseph's behavior imitated Doug's. Maybe this was her lot in life, to have temporary relationships, and not find a man who truly cared afterward, let alone love for the rest of her life. Insecurity seeped into her awareness, and she swallowed a thick knot of discouragement. So much for fulfilling every fantasy and she had damn well looked forward to searching the dark corners of her convictions. She stood, gathered Joseph's empty bowl and bolted to the cabin.

She knocked on the door, and no one answered. Concerned for their welfare, but aware they might be resting, she tiptoed inside. "Elizabeth? Mrs. Dibello?" She meandered to the familiar bedroom.

"I didn't realize you were still here." The new mother fidgeted to a sitting position with her back against the wooden headboard. Cheyenne poured fresh water into a cup from the glazed pitcher, and extended her hand. "Here you go."

She sipped and cradled the glassware with her palm. "I want to thank you for cleaning up after Elizabeth, and most of all for helping Andrew and me. We wouldn't have survived without you."

"It was an honor, Mrs. Dibello."

"Please, call me Mary."

Cheyenne smiled at her kindness, but was worried for Mary's daughter. "Where's Elizabeth?"

"She's staying with my neighbor, Helen, for a few days. I sent my milk cow because I don't have the strength to attend Daisy twice a day. Helen is a sweet woman, she brought food and clean diapers." Mary laughed, then sobered. "I guess she knew what I needed."

There was something to be said about the barter system and life's simplicities. Mary's head tilted to one side, as though searching for something behind her. "Good morning, Dr. Westerly."

In Joseph's presence, Cheyenne gulped down the uncomfortable sensations streaming through her system. While memories of Joseph making love to her by the tree and in the barn surfaced, the heat of embarrassment climbed from her neck to the top of her head. Cheyenne wished she could blame Joseph for using her, but she couldn't. He was a good man, just not interested in her. When would she learn, men didn't want her type, whatever that was. "I need to get going. It was nice meeting you, Mary, and I'm glad you're better."

Cheyenne pivoted and nodded at Joseph. "I wish you well, Dr. Westerly." She strolled from the bedroom even though she wanted to run. Once she cleared the outside door, she darted off the porch, jumped over mud puddles as though they were track hurdles and dashed for the lake. Maybe the run would burn off her frustration, and a swim in the cool water would remove her head from her ass, because somewhere along the line, she lost it up there.

Forty minutes later on the lake's shore, she bent at her waist and rested her palms on her knees, struggling for more oxygen. When her heart rate lowered, she stripped and rushed into the spring-fed pond. As the bitter cold encased her skin, goose bumps rose over her flesh. She inhaled, then dove under the surface. By the time she reached the other side, her teeth chattered, and her muscles didn't respond well to her commands. She inched up the bank and fell onto the soft grass face first.

The afternoon sun radiated the needed warmth. She laid her head onto her crossed arms, letting the soothing heat erase the fear of being alone in a decade she knew nothing about, but she'd figure it out. Soon, her insecurities calmed, and her thoughts quieted.

Chapter Five

Rocket lumbered on the path they had taken yesterday. Joseph would take a quick bath in the lake next to the place he had made love to his Indian Princess. He gazed into the last vestiges of light in the western sky. A red-tailed hawk circled, then plunged toward the ground and launched back into flight with a field mouse squiggling in the bird of prey's talons. Within his peripheral vision, an image caught his attention, and he yanked his focus back.

Cheyenne's naked frame lay prone, stretched the full length on the grassy bank. Her rear shifted slightly, but didn't awaken. He had to admit, Cheyenne's alluring body pleased him, her sharp mind amused him, and her lovely spirit appealed to him. At what moment did he permit her to cast her spell and enrich his life to the point he missed her presence?

When she departed Mrs. Dibello's, leaving his ass with a formal goodbye, his heart sunk to the pits of hell. He suffered like the field mouse in the hawk's claws, struggling to take his last breath before death was served. He had stumbled and stuttered, even Mrs. Dibello noticed. The new mom assured him to go after Miss Clark, and that

Pale With Color

Cheyenne loved him. Mary articulated further, she could see it in Cheyenne's transparent eyes, the window to her soul. He dismissed Mrs. Dibello's comment, but the longer he dwelled on Cheyenne leaving without an explanation, anger had set in.

His frustration delivered a cord of firewood for Mrs. Dibello. Exhausted from the labor, he said goodbye and trekked toward Gettysburg. He suspected Cheyenne would be at their tree waiting for the portal to open, but he was wrong.

He dismounted off of Rocket, dropped the reins, and gained her clothes on his way over to Cheyenne's sleeping form. The nearby trees rustled, and the breeze confirmed the temperature had dropped dramatically. Cheyenne stirred.

How would he to turn the tide of events his way? He didn't want to lose her, but if she didn't want him, he'd let her go. He had heard of dying a slow death because of a lost love, and in his estimation, the notion was a pile of horse shit. One thing he understood, he had an astronomical amount of affection for this woman; however, he wasn't sure if he could call it love. Nevertheless, he did recognize, his heart would break and his soul confined to the fiery depths of hell if Cheyenne didn't return the same sentiment to some degree.

Walk in my boots had a whole new meaning. He lowered, sat on his haunches, and lightly shook Cheyenne's shoulder. "You better get up and dress before you catch pneumonia."

Her face scrunched in agitation and her eyes opened. "Ah."

He placed his hand over her mouth. Her scream

could have carried for miles. He surveyed a three hundred and sixty degree circumference. There were plenty of rebel rousers raping and pillaging, and he had to be careful. The true soldiers were with their regiments marching to the next battle.

Once Cheyenne roused, she recognized him, and anger blazed from her gaze. She swiped his palm to the side, snatched her clothes from his hand, and scrambled to put them on.

Nothing. He sighed with relief and peered back at Cheyenne fully clothed, standing with her hand on one hip, giving him a go-to-hell look. He inwardly chuckled. Mrs. Dibello was right. "I missed you my Indian Princess."

She crossed her arms. "Don't say things you don't mean. It's not becoming of an officer."

"I've never lied to you. Something else is bothering you..." He stepped toward her, hoping she wouldn't back away. She listed in his direction.

He sidled closer, then strode to her and hauled her into his arms. She willingly clutched him in return. She sniffled, and he froze. Was he wrong? Maybe, when they had made love, he repulsed her or God forbid hurt her.

"I'm sorry...I have self-doubt that overwhelms me at times."

"We all do." He rubbed his palm up and down the length of her spine. "Let's get Rocket and settle down for the night in the copse of trees. We'll be hidden from any marauders."

She nodded. "I'd like to explain and I hope you'll understand."

"Of course, I will." He secretly despaired. Her

revelations may not be what he wanted to hear. "I'll catch up with you. I need to bathe."

Joseph grabbed the soap and cloth from the saddlebag, stripped, and entered the frigid water. The ritual didn't take long. Cleaned and dressed, he gathered the horse, lumbered deep inside the woods, and approached a small open area between several trees and evergreens, then halted. "No campfire. We can't take any chances."

He suspended the canteen on a tree limb, slipped the blanket off of Rocket and laid the cover down on the ground. Mrs. Dibello insisted on giving him a handmade quilt she had made for her husband, vowing it would only remind her of her husband's death. He unfurled the bedding and used his saddle bags as pillows.

Once hunkered between the blankets, Cheyenne snuggled against him. He loved the sensation of her touch, her feminine aroma, and most of all, how she tasted.

He waited. She didn't need him imposing his opinions, either she was ready to talk or not. If she was, he'd listen with an open mind, and would still love her, no matter what she said, good or bad. Wow, he had said love, again, could it be? The answer was an emphatic yes.

"When I think about it now, I'm embarrassed of the way I acted. With me being in...unusual circumstances, I wanted to have a normal dinner conversation. Kind of stupid. I'm sorry."

Puzzled by what she didn't say, he remained quiet.

"You're not going to accept my apology?" She

hiked the weight of her upper torso onto her forearm.

He sought for a soft tone. "I understand your desire to hold onto something *normal*, especially in our situations, but I don't believe you're being forthright."

She quieted, then placed her cheek on his chest. Several minutes past before she nestled onto his shoulder. "You're right, I'm not," she whispered. Her warm breath caressed his neck.

"I had an ex-fiancé, who wasn't very nice. You did something that reminded me of him. After we made love, we didn't hold each other very long because we were both famished. We dressed and ate without talking to one another. I know you have a lot on your mind, but I asked you a question and you never answered. I was hurt, and I disappeared without considering if *you* needed to talk. Rather than facing rejection or staying to help you, I ran away. I haven't done that in quite a while. I really have come a long way since Doug, except for today."

Pleased she confided in him, he hugged his Indian Princess. He guided her mouth to his and kissed Cheyenne. "I too have run on numerous occasions. From the countless responsibilities that fell on my shoulders when my parents and little brother died to the scores of want-to-be brides chasing after me for my money, merely to mention two. I do have a tendency to dwell in my own thoughts and not share them. I've never had anyone to impart them to—"

"I should've kept my mouth shut. I didn't mean

to infringe on your privacy. I'll be gone soon." She rose to a sitting position and wrapped her arms around her knees.

"Until now." He studied her profile in the moonlight.

"Are you manipulating me knowing I'll be leaving in a few days?" She stared off into the dark night that encapsulated them. The tree limbs and the boughs of the evergreens swayed in the gentle wind.

"No. I've fallen in love with you. I can't explain how or the rationality behind the emotion, but I'm assuming there isn't any logic to it."

She laughed out loud.

Out of all the reactions he envisioned her having, amusement was not one of them. Cheyenne clambered on top of his stomach and covered his face with kisses, still giggling. She stopped. Her gaze connected with his, and the plea implored him to give her what she wanted. "Of course, I'll make the sweetest love to you, my Indian Princess." And his cock rose, ready for the celebration.

As she plucked each article of her clothing off one by one, he mirrored her, except when it came to the new bra. He really liked that piece of fabric. The molded material pushed her breasts together similar to the corsets women wore today to get men's attention, which it did, but he wanted them only for himself. He didn't share. "Are these exclusively for me?" He held one breast in each hand.

"Only for you." She lowered her right breast until he fastened onto her nipple.

He suckled, then laved. When he released her, she shimmied down to his knees, bent forward, gently guided his cock into her mouth and sucked while her hands massaged his balls. His head jerked back, holding on to his sanity and his orgasm. Her divine tongue abstained from naivety, and she lapped his length from top to bottom. Her mouth enclosed over both of his balls, and damn, her tongue could dance.

Chapter Six

"Ride me." Joseph choked on his words.

Cheyenne licked one more time, then released him. She straddled his hips and gradually lowered onto his cock, taking an inch, then rising to the tip. His face appeared as though she tortured him. She sunk another small increment, and lifted. His thumb dipped into her essence, then rubbed her clit, slowly, lightly. She wanted more. She grasped his wrist and directed him, but he refused her guidance.

"You get what you give." His left eyebrow rose.

She slammed down, and his cock touched her cervix. She panted, absorbing the amazing pleasure pain. The power he gave her buzzed through her blood, spreading to every nerve ending, and the glorious feeling empowered her to fully open her heart and let him in. "I love you." While she rode his cock to show him how much, he played with her clit and offered his devotion to one nipple, then the other.

Her orgasm charged her forward in time to when she was happy and content, and she recognized the analogy. The parallel was synonymous with how Joseph had touched her life and became an integral part. As she entered the present, no wait, was it back...she giggled at the absurd attempt to measure the breadth of time and space.

He gently rolled her onto her back, and spread her legs with one knee. His right arm held his weight and with his left, he guided his rigid cock to her opening. In one plunge with his hips, he filled her. He waited several seconds to let her acclimate to his size. Joseph's engorged cock was huge, but not so big she had trouble. The warmth and love he shared completed her in a strange, crazy kind of way. Joseph said it best, love wasn't logical.

Joseph's advances and withdrawals remained tender, affectionate, and very close to worshipping. He retreated to the tip of his cock, then plunged to the hilt, and with each completed stroke, he'd kissed her lips, neck, and chin, suckled her nipple and earlobe. When he'd fully seated his velvet cock inside her, she squeezed her inner muscles, conveying she appreciated every little detail of how he made love.

He rolled his hips and rubbed her clit with his pelvic bone. The exquisite pressure built a blazing fire deep within. And with every withdrawal, he scraped her G-spot, adding fuel to the raging inferno. No man had ever made love to her this way, with only her pleasure in mind. He always made sure she had her climax before his, such a gentleman in every way.

Just as her thought sailed into the eternal space of karma, his arms lifted her knees until her legs rested over his shoulders. He scooted forward, and his regard asked if she was all right. She nodded, and his gaze trailed his hands as they slid down her inner thighs to her clit. He laid his cock between her feminine folds, and flexed his hips, adding pressure with his palm. With each stroke, he rasped against her bud while teasing her opening. Captured by the erotic sensations, she joined his rhythm.

Her fingers found his balls, and she gently rolled his sac. He groaned. *Bingo.* In one stroke, he filled her again. As his hips pistoned, her breasts jostled and the coarse hair on his chest rubbed against her nipples. Her turgid tips tingled. With each advance and retreat, her pinnacle was in sight.

His thumb and forefinger clasped her clit, and he tweaked her bundle of nerves. Her orgasm launched. While she pulsed from her release, she was semi-aware Joseph sustained his vigil, slamming his cock against her G-spot, and his fingers weaving their magic. He moaned, and his warm essence saturated her channel. After his last shudder and several deep breaths, he gradually withdrew, rubbed her legs, and carefully lowered them.

When he reclined beside her, Joseph tugged her into his embrace. He remembered that she wanted to be held after making love. She didn't think it was possible that love grew with each passing moment, but Joseph demonstrated his devotion through actions.

How could he fill her cup when the glass was already full? Extra affections should overflow, but she learned something about the emotion and Joseph. He didn't care how much she already had, he kept giving, and she had the power to hold his passion close to her heart for all of eternity.

He hugged her. "Let me up and I'll grab the canteen."

She rolled for the needed space. He rose, and the moonlight lit his path. His sexy butt flexed with each step.

"Yum." She didn't mean to say that out loud.

He arched his spine and wiggled his ass.

"You're good." Her gaze clung to the delicious sight, then something caught her eye. On Joseph's lower back, a distinctive birthmark in the shape of a ship's anchor moored right above his buttocks. He returned with his canteen, dug a cloth out of one side of his saddle bag, and soaked the material. He attentively cleansed her, then himself.

"I love your birthmark."

He stilled. "Do you find it offensive?"

"Not at all."

A smile crossed his face. "I consider my mark a talisman of sorts. It reminds me of home." His gaze landed on something behind her. His eyes softened as though remembering a cherished recollection. "All the majestic ships anchored in the distance and the surf breaking onto the shore."

"A lucky charm? You're smack dab in the middle of a war."

His gaze connected with hers. "I'm still alive and you are part of my life. How lucky can I get?"

"Are you sure I'm a windfall of magic? I'll be leaving shortly." She didn't want to think about returning home without Joseph, but she had to. "All I see coming down the road is hurt and anguish. Don't get me wrong, I'm holding onto everything you are giving me, your touch, your love, and the wonderful memories."

"Then stay and marry me. I'll give you a beautiful house beside the ocean, fill our home with children, and make sure you survive to see your grandchildren."

She gulped down the bevy of emotions swirling inside her. Could she make it in this era or would she die when her next cold changed into a bacterial infection, which could become a killer since antibiotics hadn't been discovered yet.

Would her friends miss her, mourn her death or worse yet, never have closure because her body wasn't found? Chris, her brother, had died several years ago so she didn't have any other close family members. Then there was Paul, her college friend and business partner, he would take over their company. She didn't see a problem there.

Should she marry the love of her life? Joseph was the only man who listened to her wishes and desires, who not only cared for her basic needs, but intuited she had major emotional hurdles to overcome. What other guy in her life, besides Paul, cared about her heart and spirit? The answer was no one. But this was a different age, which created other questions.

"You understand women in the twenty-first century not only have children, but work, vote, have a say in every decision, plus we wear pants, shorts, tank tops and bikini swimsuits. I'm no different. I'd stand out and be an embarrassment to you. It may sound all cute now, but after a while, you'd want me to conform.

"If I didn't change, you'd resent me. And if I gave up my identity, eventually, I'd get angry and begrudge the fact you changed your mind. Our children would know bitterness and that's not a suitable situation for you, me, or anyone."

Still kneeling in front of her naked, his eyebrows furrowed, he nodded solemnly, then his head tilted back and laughed. He fell on his rear and kicked out his legs. His feet surrounded her waist, he lifted her onto him, and he dropped onto his back, taking her with him. She rested on his chest, with her mouth mere inches from his, exchanging each other's breath. His mirth passed, and his gaze teased her serious inquisition.

"Damn, you have a lot on your mind." He tapped her temple. "I can see you will be into everything. I'm sorry, women can't vote, but maybe, without altering destiny, you could help change things for the better. I don't need to work, but I want to so I understand your desires. I can't imagine sitting on my..." He cleared his throat. "Doing nothing all day. As for clothes, you can wear anything you damn well please. Hell, you might start a new fashion trend."

He kissed her nose, trailing from the tip to the curve of her mouth. "Whatever your dreams are, I want to be a part of them. Give me the pleasure of sharing your aspirations, interweaving your goals with mine, and all your wishes and hopes into my life."

"Are you for real? Or am I delusional? Will I wake up from this dream in my twenty-first century bed...without you? Wondering whether you really existed?"

He fumbled with one of his silver necklaces she had wound around her finger earlier. A pendent dangled from each chain. When he put the two jagged edges together, a picture emerged. The intricate detailing captured her imagination. A beautiful Victorian house perched high on a cliff with a fence encircling the large home, and a sign caught her eye hanging on a charming entry gate, 'This is only one stop in our sojourn.' Surrounding the estate was an ocean with a cove. "It's exquisite. Separately, you can't tell what the picture is but together everything comes into focus. How did the artist do that?"

"I casted a number of dies." He chuckled.

"You crafted these?" Mesmerized by his artistic capabilities, she appreciated the depiction. "This is your home?"

"Ours." He cupped her hand and deposited the keepsake into her palm. "This is the other half of my heart, wear this, so in death, I can find you whenever I cross over." She fisted her hand, holding onto his gift as if it were her last breath. He pried open her fingers, lifted the necklace, and attached the token at her nape.

"I'll keep it on forever." She fingered the symbol of their eternal promise to one another.

"When we get back to Gettysburg, we'll get married and I'll commission a small box for you." He shrugged. "Or I'll make it myself, so you'll know, you're not …how did you say it? Delusional or in a dream."

She smiled. He wanted and trusted her,

believed the crazy situation she was in before she could accept the circumstances. Above all, he loved her, and she desired to bestow the same passionate pledges. "Yes, I'll do it. I'll marry you."

"Now, come here, my future wife, we've got some celebrating to do."

The next morning, after a quick bath in the lake, they returned to their campsite. Joseph checked Rocket's hooves, then he mounted the powerful stud. She climbed on top of a boulder, he clasped her forearm and assisted her onto the horse, taking the same position in front of him like she had the other day.

He clicked his tongue, and Rocket danced forward. Joseph gently prodded Cheyenne to bend at the waist, forcing her to hug the horse's neck, while branches skimmed over their backs. They cleared the woods, and Rocket changed the pace to a gallop. Sunlight reflected off the lake's surface, and she hid her eyes in the horse's mane.

Images of the man at the reenactment crowded her memory. Again, the same familiarity washed over her senses. What she had once considered a peculiar gaze was now extraordinary and loving. How was it possible to understand the ease of intimacy with a stranger? She shivered.

"You trembled, are you all right?" Joseph straightened his spine, laid the reins on Rocket's right side; the stallion steered west and slowed to a walk.

"I'd give my next meal for my shades, but I forgot them in your tent." She raised into a sitting position.

"Shades?"

"Sunglasses." Her fingers drew the shape of the frames.

"Ah. I hope you weren't attached to your painted spectacles, because I bet they're gone. One of the things I noticed, they're not metal. I read something about an inventor having that type of material at the Great Exhibition in London. It's going on now. I envisioned it to be like your...sunglasses. Damn, I would've gone had it not been for this cursed war. But then, we wouldn't have met."

She patted his leg. "It's made of a different material. The generic term is plastic."

"Plastic. It's exciting to hear about what our children's grandchildren will be experiencing. What about the medical field?"

"Lots of milestones. I noticed you already do this, but the best thing you could do for the injured is to tell your colleagues about washing their hands with soap and use a brush under their fingernails before and after every patient, no matter what. It cuts down on the inadvertent transfer of tiny microorganisms which causes disease."

"I've tried, but there was only one doctor who accepted my advice. That's little consolation for the many patients we attend."

Joseph shuddered, and she changed the subject. "What's your favorite color?"

"The same shade as your eyes. Aquamarine. Yours?"

She twisted to face Joseph, her gaze locked on his, she found her choice. "Emerald green."

He closed the distance, and his warm lips met hers. When Joseph straightened, he whispered, "Now, tell me your favorite flower."

"Wildflowers. And thistles are beautiful too. Your turn."

"You."

"That's not an answer."

Chapter Seven

"Good morning, my beautiful wife." Joseph kissed her, then made the sweetest love to her. His thrusts were given with reverence, and the withdrawals were a promise that he'd return.

After post coital bonding and cleansing, Joseph bounced out of bed, dressed, and peered out the inn's window. "I've been ordered to go back to Wheatfield today and check the grounds for any of our soldier's personal effects. Actually, after three days of battle and all the commotion, I'm to make sure there aren't any notes that would give away any military secrets. I can't imagine finding anything. Want to come with me?"

"Love to."

"Then I have to join my regiment."

Tears inundated her eyes. "You could be killed. Besides, a week honeymoon isn't long enough. Can't you ask for another extension?"

"The men need me. Besides, we agreed on this together."

"I still don't have to like it." She rested her spine against one of the brass posts of the headboard.

"Mr. Cromwell, our butler, will meet you at the train station. I've contacted my solicitor to initiate several accounts. You'll have access to the funds for the house, staff and the necessaries and one which is exclusively yours, in gold as well as coin."

He strolled to the bedside, sat and gathered her into his arms. "I'll return. You can count on it."

Joseph was safe now, but doctors were known to become prisoners of war too. She shivered, not wanting to think about the revolting conditions he'd have to endure. "I can be ready in about twenty minutes."

"I'll meet you downstairs." He rose and strode out of the room.

She whisked the covers off, climbed out and made the bed. While brushing her teeth, she fingered the wildflower bouquet with the singular thistle Joseph had picked. She was glad she had packed several toiletry items, and super happy she shared Joseph's life as his wife. With her morning absolutions finished, she dressed, grabbed her backpack, and meandered downstairs.

"Mrs. Westerly, over here."

Her gaze searched for the bass voice she fell in love with, and found Joseph at a table for two with a breakfast plate. Food was scarce, but somehow the innkeepers, Mr. and Mrs. MacIntyre, provided for everyone.

Mrs. MacIntyre held a pitcher in each hand. She lifted one several inches higher than the other. "Eh?"

"No, ma'am." Cheyenne's cheeks warmed and shook her head once. At the beginning of the week, Mrs. MacIntyre offered her milk. She'd taken a sip and couldn't palate the stuff. Mrs. MacIntyre told all the patrons, Cheyenne needed to drink the nourishing sustenance, because she could be carrying Dr. Westerly's child. Since then, every morning, Mrs. MacIntyre extended her another chance to improve the baby's odds for a healthy life.

"You still have the beautiful blush of a new bride." Mrs. MacIntyre filled her glass with water, and scurried off to refill another customer's mug.

"That's because she still is." Mr. MacIntyre cleaned the bar with a wet rag, and nodded at Joseph.

Joseph winked at Cheyenne and grinned. There it was again. The ability to make her feel instantly at ease. "It's possible." His emerald eyes danced. "Our baby could be growing in you, right now."

"I told you about—"

"Twenty-first century birth control…Even you quoted it's not one-hundred percent effective."

"True."

Under the table, he rubbed his palm over her belly. "Then let me have my illusion, before I head back into this wretched war. When things get bad and I see death and destruction, I can hold onto the notion when the dust settles, our child will be better off."

"Anything is possible."

"Ready to go?"

"Whenever you are."

****

As Cheyenne walked hand in hand with Joseph, the wheat field appeared different; their beautiful tree several yards away seemed altered, although she couldn't attribute a reason for it. She hadn't been back since they'd left for Mrs. Dibello's, but Joseph had. Between the rain and all the people helping to bury the soldiers, they hadn't found any personal items or anything to be construed as military secrets.

The whole situation saddened her that she couldn't share the history, because passing any type of information would affect destiny. The repercussions would change the course of the country's future, and the citizen's lives, even her own. The idea of not having Joseph scared her into keeping her mouth shut.

Without any warning, Miss Johnson on Rocket barreled through the curtain of time and galloped away from them.

"Well, I'll be damned. That's how she prevented her horse from being conscripted...Do you think she's from your time?"

She couldn't explain the tug. If Miss Johnson could come and go, why couldn't they do it too? Together.

He squeezed her palm. "You okay?"

"Yeah."

"But"

"How did—"

"We just saw Miss Johnson and her horse appear and ride out of here. You're wondering whether you made the right decision in marrying me. Damn, what have I done?"

"That's not it." Chill bumps rose over her flesh. "Why couldn't we travel back and forth, at least until the war ends?"

"I can't walk away from the men. I have a duty, and they need me."

"I understand… What if something happens to you and I go back—forward—could you find me?"

Joseph halted and grasped both of her shoulders. "Don't be frightened. All of our late night talks, we both believe in the afterlife, whether in spirit form or reincarnation. So what's the big deal?"

"You believe in rebirth. The jury's still out with me."

He laughed, then his facial expression sobered. "*If* something happens to me, I'll locate you."

"Karma. Jinx." She shuddered, and shifted to his side.

A pop resonated. Joseph's muscles stiffened, and his eyes rounded in shock. "Damn." He palmed his chest and crumbled.

"*No.*" She encircled her arms around his chest and buffered his fall. Her elbows broke a fraction of their tumble. She tugged her hands from beneath him. Blood continued to spread over his shirt and he labored to breathe. "Don't you dare die on me."

He opened his eyes. "I'm not going to make this one."

"Bullshit. Tell me what to do." Her hands shook as she unbuttoned his shirt, and used the material to plug the hole.

"Blood is filling my lungs. I don't have much time. Listen to me, my Indian Princess."

She swallowed hard.

"You have a choice of where you want to live and perhaps the year."

She shook her head, not wanting to hear what he had to say, desperately wishing this horrific nightmare would end.

"Go, it's not too late." He gasped, and his lungs rattled, emphasizing how close to death he was. "Miss Johnson made it."

Rocket snorted behind her as Miss Johnson ran to the other side of Joseph and knelt. "What happened? Oh shit, you're shot. That bastard."

Joseph's eyebrows rose in response to Miss Johnson's declaration. He gasped for air, then studied Cheyenne. "I can't guarantee your safety. The solicitor hasn't sent the papers...To sign. You'd be on your own." He turned his neck slightly, coughed, and spit, bloody sputum drained from his mouth.

"Go." He coughed, again.

"NO." She shook her head violently. "I'm not going to leave you. I won't."

"I don't want you to remember me dead."

"So dying is okay?"

"No, Indian Princess. It's not." He slowly raised his hand and rubbed her belly. Take care of our little one...I love you...Remember...I'll find you." His arm dropped.

Cheyenne checked the pulse at his neck. Nothing. She embraced Joseph and kissed him. Her tears flowed down both of her cheeks and dripped onto his. Her gut heaved. She crawled several feet away and hurled.

When she finished, Miss Johnson handed her a handkerchief. She dabbed her forehead and her mouth. "Do you by any chance have a pen and paper?"

Miss Johnson gasped. "A pen? How did you know? Did you see me come through with Rocket?"

"We both did." She focused on Joseph. He laid so peaceful.

For the first time, Miss Johnson's attention was on her clothing, then her wedding band. "What year are you from?"

"Suffice it to say, the twenty-first century."

"Are you going to rat me out?"

"Your secret is safe with me."

"I have a couple of hours before the G-man shows up again. I led him to believe I was heading away from Gettysburg. He's from the government and has been trying to get my horse. When I came through, the asshole ambushed me. Obviously, he's not a good marksman or he would've got me instead of your husband. I can't let him take Rocket. It's how I take care of both of my family's, here and back home, through stud fees." Miss Johnson lowered her chin. "Leading two different lives is crazy. I can't keep up, but I can't walk away from either one of them. What do I do?" Miss Johnson's gaze pleaded for a rational answer.

Cheyenne sniffled. "I'm not one to give advice, but once you're honest with your family, both of them, I bet they'll help you solve the problems...It doesn't hurt to try."

"Okay, I'll think about it... I'm sorry to sound so crass, but where do you want to bury him? I'll help."

"By our tree."

Miss Johnson smiled tentatively and dug out of

her saddle bag several sheets of paper and a neon gel pen.

Cheyenne scribbled a note and stuffed the short letter into Joseph's pocket. Interring him was going to be the hardest thing she ever had done.

Two hours later, Cheyenne laid wildflowers with one thistle on the overturned earth and said a prayer. She thanked Miss Johnson and patted Rocket good-bye, her vision blurred from weeping.

"Anytime you want to visit his grave, come through during the phases of the Gaelic moon. Rest assured, I'll let his solicitor and Mr. Cromwell know you'll not be arriving." Miss Johnson wrapped her arms around Cheyenne and squeezed. "I'll tend his gravesite."

Could Joseph be right about the Celtic journeys? Was it possible, he'd meet her back home in the twenty-first century? The last thing she wanted to do was miss him. "I gotta go." She encouraged Miss Johnson to release her.

"I'm not so sure about the reincarnation you told me about. All I'm saying, don't be disappointed." Miss Johnson freed Cheyenne, and whisked Rocket's reins into her hands.

"He's going to come and get me." For the first time since Joseph died, she had hope.

"You better go, because at the latter part of the twenty-four hour span, the harder it will be for you to travel across. Right before the conduit closes, all the molecules condense and it's downright difficult to walk through. Especially after Dr. Westerly's death, I don't want to find out what would occur if the particles compacted with you still in between time."

"So that's what happened…" She recalled the struggle, gravity had magnified to the extent she strained every muscle to obtain forward motion, and labored to breathe.

"Godspeed." Miss Johnson nodded once.

"And to you." She blew a kiss to Joseph's grave and strode through the warp which had given her the love of her life. The weird heaviness had dissipated, and she strolled right through, trusting the Celtics would guide her to the right century.

Chapter Eight

Cheyenne entered her office, walked into her personal bathroom and flipped the light switch. The large mirror reflected her finger following the never ending circle of the wedding band. She had slipped the ring onto the chain next to the pendant Joseph had given her to quell any questions. When she had returned close to a year ago, Bethany and Paul demanded answers. She didn't have any. Both of them had suspiciously scrutinized her, but in the end, they let her have her space.

The first several weeks, she spent at home and waited for Joseph, while she counted the days in her cycle. She had traded in her car, hoping positive actions would improve her chances with destiny. One morning, fate sealed her future, her period arrived, and her heart crumbled.

Two months later, she gave up. How could she have been so stupid and naïve? Reincarnation, what a bunch of lies. Although, she clung to one truth, Joseph had loved her, but rebirth she guessed was not an option in the afterlife…or was it before?

A quick knock sounded and the door opened. "Hey." Bethany poked her head across the threshold.

She hastily dropped the necklace under her T-

Shirt and patted the precious memories close to her heart. "Good morning. What brings you by?"

Bethany sidled next to her, draped one arm around her shoulder and squeezed. "I haven't told you before, but I've seen your wedding ring and whatever the other thing is. *He* gave it to you."

It wasn't a question, merely a statement, so she remained quiet.

"I don't know exactly what happened, but it's time you moved on. It's been a year, and he's not coming back."

If Bethany only understood it was forward, Joseph wasn't coming forward, to touch, or to love her ever again. Tears welled and she blinked rapidly. "You're right."

"Are you going to going to the reenactment this year?"

Cheyenne nodded. "Of course, I always go." Bethany had a point, maybe she should say goodbye.

"Do you need some company?"

When she said her farewells, she wanted to be alone, besides she'd be horrible company. "No thanks, I...um...I—"

"I understand. Weird things happened there." Bethany's head tilted and their gazes connected through the reflection of the mirror."

"What do you mean?" Cheyenne gasped.

"Nothing... By the way, I came to tell you *the* guy is in line." Beth nudged her back, turned-tail and ran.

"I wish she'd stop that." Bethany had a bad habit of pushing her. She snatched her electric-blue apron from the hook and ambled out of the bathroom. Whoever the Mystery Man was, she liked hearing him order her special blend of Chai tea. His voice sounded like Joseph's, even his eyes were the same color.

She slipped the smock over her head and wrapped the strings around her waist—twice—then knotted them. Her appetite had been non-existent, and she lost a considerable amount of weight. Someday she was going to cut the blasted long ties, but it wouldn't be today. She strode to the front and peered into the barista's mirror which covered the length of the back wall, hoping to see the Mystery Man's emerald eyes, and his beard, a chestnut shadow, covering his masculine jaw.

Within the reflection, an open field materialized. She walked hand in hand with Joseph. He lifted Cheyenne's palms and kissed each of her fingertips. The oak tree towered above the numerous mounds of overturned dirt. She understood loved ones rested under the layers of soil, and she shuddered. Pop. The sound reverberated in her ears. She closed her eyes. Scared of what she'd see next, and at the same time rivaling her fear, the phenomenon captured her curiosity, Cheyenne peeked again, and the next image revealed Joseph dead, laying on the grass. She blinked several times, staring into the glass, and the scene vanished. She scraped her sweaty palms against her thighs. How many times would she relive Joseph's death? After a year, she expected to be over his passing. Had anyone noticed she was hallucinating? How long had she stood fixated?

Glancing to her left and right, her employees were working on the same orders before the episode began. She scanned the mirror one more time and there he was, the Mystery Man stood second in line. She pivoted and tripped over the mat. Her hands strained to catch one of the refrigerator handles, each second stretched into eternity.

She missed and fell to the floor. *Really?* She lifted her chin, squinting through her hair which covered her face in time to see Mystery Man leaning over the counter and studying her. *Crap.*

"Are you okay?" His brows furrowed.

"Disappearing would be good right about now."

"Don't move." In one effortless jump, he hefted over the work surface and landed on his feet. "Let me check you."

She gasped.

"Relax. I'm a doctor." His fingers wisped her long tresses to the side with the softest touch of any man save one, Joseph.

She grinned as heat rose from her throat to her cheeks. Why was she blushing like a school girl?

"No need to be embarrassed." One end of his mouth lifted higher than the other.

"Oh bother, the floor could open and swallow me whole and I'd welcome it."

He chuckled. "My name is Jonathan Davis, and unless I'm mistaken, yours is Cheyenne, assuming you didn't swipe someone's name tag?" His fingertips probed her neck, shoulders, then skimmed along each extremity.

"I've done a lot of things, but theft isn't one of

them."

"Glad to hear it. I can't find anything wrong. Ready to stand?"

"Sure."

Jonathan helped her rise and she wobbled. "You should sit for a while. Is there a quiet place?"

"That way." She pointed. "You can let go of me, I'm fine."

When Jonathon withdrew, she weaved and stumbled. He caught her.

"Thanks." With his support, she led the way to her office.

"Don't do anything I wouldn't do." Paul waggled his eyebrows.

"Buzz off," she ground out.

"Buzz?"

"I'm trying to be nice." Cheyenne rubbed her temple with her middle finger as she passed Paul in the hallway. Crossing the threshold with Jonathan behind her, he closed the door.

Since she'd been depressed and couldn't shake the desolation, Bethany insisted on rearranging the furniture. Positioned to the right, her desk set at an angle accepted the light from the window to enhance a positive energy flow into the room and continue its journey to the common area for the customers. On the left, the currant colored couch, loveseat, and the mahogany coffee table rested in sharp angular patterns. The arrangement required an exorbitant amount of space to her way of thinking, but she'd let Beth have her fun.

She sat on the far side of the sofa, and her hand gestured for Jonathan to pick a seat. "Make yourself comfortable."

He sank onto the middle cushion beside her.

"You're a runner." Her gaze followed the long linear line of his leg. His shorts enveloped his muscular thighs, and the dark, wispy hair was damn sensual. She journeyed higher, scouting for a tan line. *Nada.* She regarded his masculine bulge. Even if a jock strap secured his cock, he was hung very nicely. She envisioned her tongue laving Jonathan's engorged shaft, then her mouth taking him, suckling until she tasted his essence. Heat infused her core and swelled in response to her fantasy.

She shook her head to dispel the mental illusions. How could she daydream about sex with another man when she was mourning? There was still a niggling of unfaithfulness even though Joseph was gone. Didn't she just scold herself for not moving forward?

"Are you going to answer me or are you going to continue to eat me with your luscious aquamarine eyes?"

Only Joseph used those specific words to describe them. "I'm sorry, what?"

"Every morning I come here and buy your Chai tea. I take a couple of sips, throw it out, and start my run. Now why do you suppose I'd do something like that?"

"Obviously not for its inspiring and uplifting effects." She pretended to cough and hid her amusement. "Try drinking the tea, then come—" She cleared her throat, and somehow maintained a straight face. "See me."

After Jonathon's brows furrowed, his

expression brightened in understanding and grasped her innuendo. "I look forward to it." He grinned, stood, then strode the length of the room and examined the memorabilia perched on the mahogany bookcase. "I see you are a Civil War buff, especially the Battle of Gettysburg." The mirror backing reflected the sexy slant of his smile.

"I get into it." She licked her lips as she ogled his butt. "I'm heading out there to watch the reenactment. Does your ass— I mean, do you want to go with me?"

He spun toward her, and his head tilted to the side.

Surely, he was measuring her stupidity, and how fast he could get away. "I'm sorry. I've been totally out of line. I don't know what's wrong with me." She rose and extended her hand. "My name is Cheyenne Clark. After several months of your patronage, I'm pleased to finally meet you. Thank you for rescuing me, and it's time I let you get back to your run." Rescuing? Joseph had saved her on numerous occasions. How much longer would she compare every male against Joseph?

Jonathan ignored her gesture and in one swift motion, he drew her into his arms. Mental warning signals flashed in her mind, but she snuggled into his warmth and inhaled his masculine scent which smelled so familiar. His mouth hovered above the whorl of her ear. "I would go with you, but I have a meeting."

He kissed the span of her jawline until he found her lips, and he nibbled the bottom, then the top. She opened, and his tongue penetrated, electricity zinged to every nerve ending as he probed. The taste of spearmint tickled her taste buds. When he withdrew, the outline of his chestnut lashes emphasized the desire emanating from his gaze, and at the same time, a question emerged from the depths. Did he feel it too?

Cheyenne couldn't explain what happened between them. Besides Joseph's, would there be other souls she could be securely bound to through eternity? Was it possible she could learn to trust and love again? She doubted any of those scenarios.

"I have to go. What time do you get off?" Jonathan's palms covered each side of her cheeks, and he kissed the tip of her nose.

"About noon." She gripped both of his hands and lowered them. On his left ring finger, a jagged scar extended from one joint to the other. She gasped. Surely there were more people who had that type of a scar. She released him, and he strode to the door.

He grasped the handle and spun. "There are some things in this universe I can't rationalize or account for, so I accept them. Will or maybe the question is, can you? I'll be in touch." He winked, then strolled out of the room.

She plopped on the couch and reiterated his words out loud. A warm sensation inundated her heart, then a cold realization struck. "Can you?"

Paul stuck his head into her office. "I could use your help."

"Back to the real world." She rose and shook off the premonition.

At twelve-fifteen, she waved to Paul. "See you

in a few days."

"No. You're on vacation." Paul clutched each shoulder and forced her toward the door.

After returning to work, she voluntarily slogged through eighteen hours, seven days a week, since staying busy preserved her sanity. Plus, it allotted Paul the down time, because he had covered for her during the readjustment phase as she liked to call it.

"So, start vacationing. I'll see you in two weeks." Paul propelled her across the threshold.

She smacked into Jonathan's chest. "Sorry, Paul is a little overzealous to get rid of me."

"Lucky me." Jonathan slid his arm around her waist.

"Jeans and a T? I expected khaki's and a button-down shirt."

"Meetings are informal. Hungry?"

"Famished."

"What about Mama B's? We can walk there?"

"I love Italian."

At the restaurant, Mama B lavished her attention on Jonathan. The older woman escorted them to a private room. A singular table set for two graced one side, a bottle rested inside an ice bucket while condensation rolled down the stainless steel container, and a white linen towel hugged the wine. On the opposite side, the seating area faced a massive stone fireplace. A welcoming fire blazed in the hearth. Even though it was summertime, she enjoyed the flamed ambience, but that wasn't what caught her eye, beautiful vases with wildflowers covered every conceivable space and inserted in the center of each bouquet, a singular Spear thistle.

Cheyenne gasped. "How did you know?"

Jonathan placed his thumb under her chin and lifted until his gaze captured hers. "I can't explain how I know these things. I simply do."

Mama B cleared her throat.

Jonathan lowered his hand and pivoted to face their hostess. "Absolutely stunning, you've outdone yourself. Thank you from the bottom of my heart." He kissed each cheek of Mama B's, then she skittered through the door and closed it.

"How about a drink?" In his tight jeans and a black T-shirt, he seemed comfortable. He sauntered over, withdrew the bottle from the bucket, wiped it off and deftly removed the cork. He poured the Pinot Noir, handed her a glass and signaled to sit anywhere. Trembling, she sunk onto the chair at the table, and placed the cut crystal beside her plate.

"If you don't like this type of wine, I can get a different one." Jonathan folded his frame onto the seat across from her.

Everything about Jonathan was Joseph made over, from his voice, his emerald eyes, the jagged scar on his ring finger, identifying her favorite flowers, but Joseph didn't know she preferred Pinot Noir, and Jonathan did. Could Jonathan be Joseph reincarnated or was she losing her sanity?

As she clasped the stem and sipped, she quickly scanned Jonathan. If she really compared the two, Jonathan had brown hair and his physique was far different from Joseph's. Jonathan was taller, leaner, probably because he ran every day, but she had seen his muscular legs and his arms, chest, and other things bulging at all the right places. "It's perfect.

The wine, I mean."

When he swallowed, his Adam's apple bobbed. "This is the second time you've devoured me with your gaze. It's becoming a habit—"

"Sorry. I don't know what's wrong with me." She stood. This was the second time she had to apologize to Jonathan, and she understood why. Jonathan's charismatic appeal was strong. Before she considered any relationship, whether it was with Jonathan or another man, she needed to say goodbye to Joseph and release the emotional and spiritual ties that bound her.

"And I don't mind at all." He grinned.

"I'm not very good company, appreciate your offer for lunch, but—"

He rose. "Wait, don't leave…Stay." He thumbed something under his T-Shirt. "I can't figure out what's going on. I'm like two different people. I'm intact, but not whole, something is missing. And I think it's you. Don't ask me why, because I can't explain it. Let's sit on the couch and talk."

"Maybe, I can help." The words escaped. Had she lost her ever loving mind? Would he understand? Although, she wanted Jonathan to be Joseph reincarnated, he wasn't. Jonathan was too different, and even though the similarities between them were staggering, she had to get a grip on reality. Her universe had played some gruesome games, and the last thing she needed was to add bad karma to her world. She'd set Jonathan straight, tell him she wasn't the answer to his problems. She strode over and sat beside him.

Chapter Nine

Jonathan Davis stared at Cheyenne in disbelief as she weaved a story about a New Orleans's medium, and because the woman expressed her statements out loud, it influenced our cosmos. His gut told him she tried to grasp for a plausible explanation while desperately attempting to hide her true feelings. She denied the power of knowledge he had of her and their explosive attraction for each other.

There were too many coincidences to blame it on a fortune teller in a port city. When he had called the florist, he intuited Cheyenne's favorite flowers, including the thistles. Out of all the plants in the world, how in the hell did he know which ones to choose? He added this situation to the many other occurrences during his lifetime. Specifically, the one that he comprehended the intricacies of the human body and had the innate ability to diagnose before any formal education.

"Thank you for the wine and company. You take care of yourself." She patted his knee, but her hand lingered longer than a normal "we're friends" tap, then she rose and left.

He ran a hand through his hair as the light in his soul dimmed from Cheyenne's absence. His mind pleaded for a resolution to dispel the raging chaos. He stood, and paced the room.

The door opened. "Everything okay?" Mama B's hands twisted the edge of her apron, and her eyebrows furrowed with concern. "You pushed her away?" Her Italian accent resonated.

Another talk loomed in the air from the woman who raised him from the time he was eleven. He swallowed the fury burning inside, not wanting to hear her words of wisdom. Her aim had always been true and direct, focused on his vulnerable past, the one place he had no desire to reexamine.

"Ever since you saw your mom and dad killed by those wild mustangs, you've been—"

"I don't want to go there."

"I was your mom's best friend; she wouldn't want you like this."

"Is that so?"

"I love you, but all your life you have defied odds and challenged limitations. With women, after the third date, *ciao*. *Niente*. Nothing. Have you ever had—"

"None of your—"

"Kids. What am I to do with you?" She clicked her tongue. "All these years, the parade of women, I don't understand." Her hands lifted in the air as though asking for divine intervention, then just as adamantly, she dropped them to her side, and they slapped her thighs.

"I refuse to discuss my dating—"

"*Il mio piccolo...*" Her motherly gaze softened. "She's the one; I see it in your eyes."

He smiled, strode over to lady who loved him

unconditionally and kissed both of her cheeks again. "With or without the Cheyenne, I'll be back." He released her, spun for the exit, wondering where he'd locate her.

"It's time to stop running from your ghosts."

He paused at the doorway, peered over his shoulder, and considered her comment. She struck the mark once more. "The notion that Cheyenne completes me in every way is strange. I'm not sure if it's healthy, but I aim to find out." He dipped his chin goodbye.

In the parking lot, he slid into the driver's seat and cranked the engine. How in the hell would he find her? He peered at the review mirror as Cheyenne's vehicle zoomed past. He shifted into first gear, tugged on the steering wheel, punched the accelerator, and laid rubber.

Once he caught up with her, he maintained some distance between them so if Cheyenne recognized him, she wouldn't freak out. He wasn't a stalker, but he needed answers to the all his questions. The most important one, why him?

He remembered the first day he had entered C & P's Barista Café drawn by an inexplicable force. When he saw Cheyenne, he understood there was a significance, although the meaning alluded him.

She had been happy back then, but it was hard to figure out her hours. He stopped whenever he could. He ordered enough tea to float a battleship, and that's when he noticed Cheyenne had swapped her two-door coupe for a mini-van.

Ever since he encountered Cheyenne, his life had been bizarre. She would look at him with an intensity which lured him into the swirling depths of her aquamarine eyes, and at the same time, the power of her gaze generated a familiar sensation, a personal intimacy of sorts. He couldn't make sense of the perceptions, he didn't even know her.

Not too long after, her countenance had changed, and when their gazes connected, her profound sorrow tore at his soul. How was it possible to understand her grief? Once more, he begged to grasp why he yearned to celebrate Cheyenne's joy or console her when she was desolate?

Within a few more turns, he recognized where she was headed, Gettysburg National Military Park. His stomach lurched.

Bethany worked for their group and he'd discovered Bethany and Cheyenne were best friends. He'd asked the P.A. for Cheyenne's number. Before the Wheatfield reenactment started, he'd texted Cheyenne an odd name, felt compelled to do it, hoping she'd be able to explain everything. When he finally wrestled enough courage to initiate a conversation, she had disappeared. Although he didn't mean to, maybe he had scared her.

As she drove onto the grounds, he slowed and let several cars in between them. By the time he found her again, she'd walked around the lone tree where she stood a year ago. The mighty oak drew him, and he didn't understand the significance, but he let the energy lure him closer.

Even though Cheyenne's back was to him, he overheard her talking, but there wasn't anyone nearby. She traipsed around the tree, looking at the ground as though searching for something, and soon there were tears spilling down her face. Deep in his heart, he understood she mourned for someone. It was the same sentiment, she bestowed on him at her coffee bar. He couldn't bear her distress any longer and strode beside her. "Let me hold you."

She inhaled a quick breath. "What the hell are you doing here?" Cheyenne inched away from him.

He closed the distance between them. "I'm..." A strange sensation burned on his chest. He palmed the scorching pain.

"What's wrong?" She laid her hand over his, static electricity singed his flesh. She flinched and added more space.

"You feel it, too. Or you care more than you're letting on." He shadowed her steps until her back met the tree trunk. Her desire laced gaze linked to his, replacing the fear of a second ago.

He lowered his head and softly nipped her bottom lip. Her mouth opened, inviting his advances, and he kissed her thoroughly. She was so responsive to his touch. His palm found her waist, and he resisted the craving to journey farther down. A familiarity knocked at his consciousness, and he battled to understand.

Memories emerged, and he released Cheyenne. "I've made love to you against a tree, but not this one."

Cheyenne's eyes rounded in what appeared to be surprise.

"Not in the conventional sense. I fingered..." His cock lengthened, liking the idea while the tips of his ears heated with embarrassment, because he'd blurted the inexplicable recollection without thinking. And damn, he hated the red tell sign.

A strange veil encapsulated them. Cheyenne gasped and intertwined her fingers with his. "Don't be afraid."

The space around them pulsated, and she tugged his arm. He trailed Cheyenne through the flickering waves of the weighty atmosphere that was pale with color. He hesitated, but yet he discerned the answers he searched for all his life were on the other side of this phenomena.

When they emerged from the warped air flow, all the pieces of the puzzle fit together. He gazed at Cheyenne's hand. "Why aren't you wearing my wedding band?"

She yanked from his hold. "Because we're not married. You don't have a clue what's going on so leave it be." She searched the ground again. "What day and year is this? I have to find out." She raced into the woods, and he bolted after her.

"Stop." He closed the distance. She slowed a little, but continued her forward momentum. *Damn it.* He gripped both of her shoulders and lifted her. Her legs stilled, a shocked expression plastered across her beautiful face. "Will you listen to me?"

Several seconds later, Cheyenne nodded.

He gently placed her feet on the ground. "At last, I understand. Now all I have to do is convince you, my Indian Princess."

Disbelief surfaced on her face.

"Remember when I shared with you I was two distinct persons combined into one, but I didn't understand the conundrum. I'm Joseph reincarnated. I have every single memory of Joseph—I mean me—

"The history and his life... My life— My love for you. I know everything we did together. Hell now, I understand why you bought the damn minivan." Excitement and relief coursed through his blood. "I lived in a Victorian house by the ocean. My butler's name is—was—Mr. Cromwell—

"While I tended the soldiers in the hayloft, Mrs. Dibello guided you through a rough delivery and Andrew was born. Even though you were scared, you overcame your fear. I was so damn proud of you.

"On our honeymoon, Mrs. MacIntyre urged you to drink fresh milk because— Well, she assumed you were pregnant, and I wanted to believe it so badly...You were afraid our time together was a fantasy or possibly you were delusional. To belay your fears, I made a box for you and put in it your backpack—"

"Liar." Tears gathered in Cheyenne's eyes.

He had been so excited everything finally made sense that he didn't *see* his Indian Princess plunging into an emotional freefall. The pain in her gaze ripped his heart into a thousand pieces and pulverized his enthusiasm.

The sound of hooves clamored toward them. Miss Johnson reined in Rocket; dirt flew in every direction. "G-men are coming and they're out for blood. Get on. We have to try to get through, because this isn't a Gaelic moon. The only reason I can think as to why you got through is sun flares, and our passage may be closing this very second.

Rocket should be strong enough to make it."

Jonathan hoisted Cheyenne behind Miss Johnson. "Go."

"They'll kill you." Cheyenne extended her hand as lead whizzed by, pinging the foliage.

He clutched Cheyenne's forearm and swung his leg. With Cheyenne counterbalancing his weight, he maneuvered onto Rocket's rear. Miss Johnson clicked her tongue, and the horse bolted. Within several strides, they entered the conduit. Massive pressure shrouded him.

Something grazed his arm, and he forced his head to the right. A piece of lead inches ahead of his arm remained suspended like a still picture captures an increment of time. He mustered the strength and forced Cheyenne and Miss Johnson to bend forward at their waist, creating a smaller target.

Rocket whinnied a pitiful shriek then reared. He slid farther down Rocket's rump. Cheyenne slipped with him. He heaved Cheyenne forward, and her knees clung to the horse's side, but it was too late for him. He flipped over Rocket's tail, and his head hit the hard ground.

He awakened under the oak tree with Rocket's nose nudging his feet, while Cheyenne tended the wound on his arm.

"Can you hear me?" Cheyenne's gaze filled with worry. Mrs. Dibello's words rang true. Cheyenne's eyes were the window to her soul.

"Loud and clear."

"Thank God." She finished tying off the bandage, then embraced him fully.

He liked the fact she seemed relieved and loved

her hugs even more. "You were pissed at me, what changed?"

"We're alive." She grasped his shoulders and shook. The pendent on his chain tumbled from under his shirt and Cheyenne stilled. As if she had transformed into a frightened animal, she jerked to a sitting position, and removed her necklace. Her hands trembled as she seized his half, then positioned them together. "Where did you get this?"

"I've always had it, and I remember giving you the other half." His heart beat escalated at the newfound memory.

"Why are you going to such lengths to deceive me?" Anger replaced the fear of a few seconds ago.

His pulse deflated, and a sudden realization occurred. Cheyenne would never accept him as Jonathon. If their relationship progressed, she would be making love to another man. In her defense, Joseph was her husband, but could *he* live with that?

"I'm done." He twisted to his knees and stood. His T-shirt rose above the waistline of his jeans, and he yanked the hem down. Rocket scurried several paces backward wild-eyed. "Easy boy."

"You, you have Joseph's birthmark... Joseph?" Cheyenne gaped.

His point confirmed. Persona non grata. "News flash, Cheyenne. My name is Jonathan and thank God I understand everything now. I may have Joseph's memories, history, and damn it all to hell, I'm going to have to live with his love for you, but I'm still me." He jabbed his thumb to his chest for emphasis. "I have to get out of here." He pivoted to

Miss Johnson. "Thank you for saving our lives. I owe you one. By the way, check Rocket's rump, I think a bullet scraped his flesh."

He turned his head, and caught Cheyenne's gaze. "What did you once tell me? 'I wish you well.'" He spun on the ball of his foot and headed for his car with the light of his soul extinguished forever.

Chapter Ten

"I need to go, too." Cheyenne scratched one of Rocket's ears.

"Wait, what did you write and stuff into Joseph's pocket before we buried him." Miss Johnson's head tilted to the side.

"The year and my address, and it didn't do any good."

"Uh-huh. You know, it's none of my business, but you're crazy if you let Jonathan go. What's really bothering you?"

"Joseph must have had a premonition about his death… He wanted to craft a box for…let's just say the small container stood for truth and clarity, but he didn't give it to me…Jonathan swore he put the jewelry chest in my backpack. After I got home, I was so excited about Joseph coming; I threw my pack in the closet, and forgot about it."

"I'm not sure I'm following you, but it's about time you open your eyes. Everything is not what it seems." Miss Johnson climbed on Rocket. "Tell Jonathan thanks, because of his inquiry about my pop, I received word… He fell at the Battle of Shiloh." Tears tumbled down Miss Johnson's cheeks, and she wiped them away. "See ya around." She clicked her tongue. Rocket pranced sideways, then galloped west, away from Gettysburg.

****

Inside her closet, Cheyenne's hands shook as she opened her backpack and withdrew a small jewelry box inlaid with ivory, and silver, and emeralds, the same color as Joseph's eyes. She flipped the tiny clasp and opened the top. Joseph's wedding band lay on top of a piece of paper. She plucked the ring, slid it on her thumb, and carefully withdrew the parchment. With utmost care, she straightened the inked note.

My Dearest Cheyenne,

I leave my wedding band for your safe keeping, men have killed for less. If I do not make it back from the battlefield, have faith I will meet you again. I don't know who I'll be, but if a stranger somehow seems familiar, keep your heart open. However, don't be fooled, he will be his own man.

You don't have to believe in reincarnation to have my love, you will always have my heart. Don't close your eyes and keep your soul accessible.

My precious Indian Princess, I look forward to making your acquaintance, and remember to love the man for who he is.

All My Love,

Joseph

She sobbed until her swollen eyes burned. When she cooled them with a wet cloth, she reread his letter and gratitude burst through for her husband's foresight. "You've given me the sign I needed. I trust you." She cautiously slipped the paper inside the jeweled case. She grabbed her keys and bee-lined to her mini-van.

She opened the door to Mama B's Restaurant and Bar. The rotund woman smiled, then pointed. Luckily, she had guessed right. A miniscule amount of relief trickled down her spine, but her temples throbbed from the overwhelming tension coursing through her body. How was this going to play out? She traversed the room, zigzagging in between the patrons sitting in their chairs. She crossed the threshold into the private room.

Occupying the middle cushion on the couch, Jonathan had one foot propped on the coffee table with a drink in his hand, the glass rested against his jeaned thigh. He stared at the dying embers in the fireplace. "Mrs. Westerly, how can I help you?"

"How did you know it was me?" She closed the distance until she stood beside him.

He shrugged one shoulder. "You're part of me whether I like it or not."

"Do you mind if I have some wine?"

"Knock yourself out."

She strode to the table, filled a goblet and sat, wrangling over the idea that it may be too late. "I came to apologize."

"No need." His head tilted back, and he downed his drink.

Tears gathered, and she battled against all the emotions ripping her apart. "I found Joseph's jewelry box and the note."

"Great, so now you agree I'm not a liar, mission accomplished." He stood and set the empty highball glass on the mantel.

"When you left the battlefield this afternoon, you quoted what I had told Joseph at Mrs.

Dibello's. My feelings were hurt and I lashed out. I'm not trying to justify my actions; however I guess as human beings, we do have a tendency to hurt one another."

"I've had my fill of bizarre puzzles to last a lifetime. What are you trying to say and what do you want?"

"To get to know you better." Nervous energy ripped through her system.

"No, you want Joseph." He crossed his arms over his chest; the psychological barrier slapped her face.

"The note in the jewelry box. Think about what Joseph wrote and his instructions to me." How could she convince Jonathan she understood he lead an independent life from Joseph's? After reading the letter, a peace settled inside her soul. Joseph would return, and he invited her to keep her heart open. Jonathan had parts of Joseph, but Jonathan had unrelated experiences, creating a distinctive personality, a unique character, and a more diverse person. "When I compared the two of you, I failed you both."

"Cheyenne—"

"I admit, you are your own man in so many different ways."

"Name them." His agitated taunt cut through her.

"You're a runner, very athletic, and not particularly fond of horses."

"How did—"

"We were being chased by men, and they were shooting at us. You hesitated to get on Rocket."

"I was concerned for you and Miss Johnson's safety." Crimson tinged the tips of his ears.

"Ha, I know better—"

"You don't know—"

"You see what you want and go after it." She quickly added to the list.

He raised both brows in bold defiance, his red tells vanished.

"In my office, we had just met, and you kissed me. No one else affected me…the way you did." She silently called upon the cosmos for help. As she remembered the desire in his gaze and his touch, her mouth watered for more of his attention.

A deadly smirk appeared, she was losing ground, and it pissed her off. "Jonathan Davis, would you listen to me?" She vaulted from her seat and the chair crashed to the floor.

"What did you call me?"

"Did you change your name or is it still Jonathan Davis?" She placed a hand on each hip to emphasize her anger.

When he smiled, his arms relaxed and stalked toward her. "Yeah, it is. But this is the last time I'm going to ask you. What do you want?" He towered above her, his gaze challenging.

Was the slant of his mouth a positive sign? She stood her ground, not wavering. "You."

"Ditto, my Indian Princess." Jonathan drew her into his embrace and squeezed.

Chapter Eleven

One Year Later

"So what did the doctor say, Mrs. Davis?" Excitement surged through Jonathan's veins.

"You want me to tell you over the phone?" Cheyenne's voice echoed over the speaker in his office.

The traffic noise overshadowed her words. "Nope. Come by here. I have a surprise for you, a celebration of sorts."

"I'm a block from you. You remember how I'm dressed, right? Jeans, T-shirt, and tennis shoes."

"How could I forget? Those are the same clothes you had on when I first met you, and I had the luxury of stripping off." He chuckled.

"You are full of it."

"Is that so?"

She wheeled into a parking space. He waited as she slid out of the van and moseyed over.

"What do you have behind your back?"

"Something for you." He presented her with her favorite wildflower bouquet and this time, two thistles were centered.

"Two? Is there a special significance for the number?"

"Maybe so." He opened the passenger door of

his vehicle.

An hour later, he turned onto a grassy lane, down shifted and maneuvered up the mountain. He hoped she'd come to love this piece of land like he did. On top of the ridge, he parked. He snatched the picnic basket from the back, and slung the blanket over his arm. With his free hand, he assisted Cheyenne out of his new truck.

"You didn't have to sell your sports car." She squeezed his fingers.

"It's a mode of transportation, not a lifestyle. Besides, I wouldn't have driven it up this mountain."

"Hill." She laughed, and laced her fingers with his.

"Considering my early years were spent on the plains, I call it a mountain."

The lone oak tree stood tall, but there were several others nearby, and the smell of fresh cut grass permeated the air. He spread the blanket on the ground, plopped the basket on a corner, and helped Cheyenne sit in the middle of the quilt.

"Okay, tell me." He lowered his ass across from her, spread eagled both legs encompassing Cheyenne's, leaned back and let his palms take his weight. "What's going on?"

"You go first." She was making him wait; lucky for her, he had patience.

"Do you like this place?"

"It's beautiful. We're not trespassing are we?" Worry emanated from her gaze.

"No. Do you like the tree?"

"I do. It reminds me of our beginning." The

apprehension morphed into adoration.

"What do you think of the view?"

"Amazing... All right Davis, quit stalling." Cheyenne's gaze probed his with suspicion.

"This is ours, if you want it to be." He mentally crossed his fingers.

"Really?" Her countenance changed to excitement.

"I signed a letter of intent and included a deposit. If you like it, I can take you tomorrow and seal the deal."

"Like? I love this place, it's perfect." She tilted her head and her lips smirked with a hint of devilry. "Okay, give. What's with the two thistles?"

He chuckled at her open expressions, even in conversation, she was responsive. "Each one represents the person who has my heart and soul. Since we have a little one on the way, the bouquet required two."

She cleared her throat. "You need to add another."

His breath caught. "Are you serious?" He gulped more air.

She nodded.

He shoved off his hands, crawled to the love of his life, crept up her legs, and lowered her back to the ground. Keeping his weight off of her belly, he rested on one elbow and kissed her thoroughly. When he finished, he palmed the tiny bump, sliding his hand over her tummy. "Part of me waited over a hundred and fifty years for a baby."

"And the other part?"

"I'm the lucky bastard that gets the pleasure of

expanding our family." He waggled his eyebrows.

About Susan JP Owens...

Susan JP Owens lives on a ranch in Texas with her awesome husband. After work and leaving the dangerous & sizzlin' hot world of her romance stories, Susan enjoys skydiving, the great outdoors and a fine glass of wine.

Connect with Susan on the Web!

Email: Susan@SusanJPOwens.com
Website: www.SusanJPOwens.com
Follow on Twitter: @SusanJPOwens
Facebook: https://www.facebook.com/pages/Susan-JP-Owens-Author/241228112562016?ref=hl

Other Titles by Susan JP Owens

The Beginning Comes Quietly
Walking Into Her Heart

Made in the USA
Charleston, SC
01 September 2015